A Nanny for the Rancher's Twins

Heidi Main

LOVE INSPIRED®

INSPIRATIONAL ROMANCE

Recycling programs
for this product may
not exist in your area.

ISBN-13: 978-1-335-58613-1

A Nanny for the Rancher's Twins

Copyright © 2022 by Heidi Main

For questions and comments about the quality of this book, please contact us
at CustomerService@Harlequin.com.

Love Inspired
22 Adelaide St. West, 41st Floor
Toronto, Ontario M5H 4E3, Canada
www.LoveInspired.com

Printed in U.S.A.

"I built my house, you know. I could help you.

"I mean, if you'd reconsider and watch Tori and Zoe for me."

No way was Laney going to watch a pair of three-year-olds, even if they were adorable. "You've got to have other childcare options than me."

Ethan shook his head. "You're kind of my last hope."

"But we barely know each other."

"Yesterday you engaged with them like a pro. I think you'd do a fine job watching my girls. I was thinking you could nanny them until eleven. My mother will watch them later in the afternoons, so I can help you most days with the renovations, say from three to six? I'll do whatever you tell me to do." He moved to the porch and held open the door for her.

He needed help, she needed help. It was a simple exchange of services. Taking care of his sweet girls would not put her independence in peril.

Maybe she should consider his idea. "Okay, let's give this a try."

Heidi Main writes sweet inspirational romance novels set in small towns. Though she lives in central North Carolina's suburbs, she dreams of acreage and horseback riding, which is why her novels include wide-open ranches and horses. Before starting her writing career, Heidi worked with computers and taught Jazzercise. A perfect Saturday is lounging on the deck with her husband and watching the many birds in their backyard. Learn more about her books at www.heidimain.com.

Books by Heidi Main

Love Inspired

A Nanny for the Rancher's Twins

Visit the Author Profile page at LoveInspired.com.

Trust in the Lord with all thine heart;
and lean not unto thine own understanding.
In all thy ways acknowledge him,
and he shall direct thy paths.
—*Proverbs* 3:5–6

To God be the glory.

Acknowledgments

Rich—thank you for always being there,
for supporting this wild dream of mine
and encouraging me every step along the way.
I love you.

Ashlyn—thank you for being
my biggest cheerleader. Elephant shoes.

Authors Mindy, Tina, Sami, Megan
and Shellie—thank you for pushing me to
make this story, and my writing, better.

To my agent, Tamela, and my editor, Melissa—
thank you for making my dream of
writing books come true.

Chapter One

Laney Taylor stepped out of her sedan and breathed in the earthy Texas air. She'd never imagined she might one day live in Serenity, her childhood happy place.

Shielding her eyes from the hot sun, she admired the massive cattle-dotted pastures of the Triple C Ranch, those carefree summers of her adolescence rushing back to her. Julys spent at her aunt and uncle's nearby ranch, and here at the Triple C running around with the McCaw kids, were the high point of her year. An opportunity to feel part of a real family. To feel valued, loved and cherished.

Horses neighed in the background as she rolled her shoulders, pushing away the tension of the tedious six-hour drive. A drive she hoped to never make again. If things went according to plan, Serenity was now her home. She could hardly wait to settle in at the property she'd inherited from her aunt and uncle and begin the remodel that would mark Willow Creek Ranch's transformation from cattle ranch to rustic wedding venue.

As she walked to the McCaws' house, Laney's white statement sneakers crunched over the gravel parking lot. No doubt everyone at Uncle Arthur and Aunt Alice's memorial service, including Cora McCaw, thought her rude for running out the moment it ended. At twenty-eight, Laney should be able to hold her emotions together, but her grief during the service had overwhelmed her, and she couldn't bear the thought of facing anyone. So, she got in her car and fled back to San Antonio like a scared child without so much as thanking anyone for coming.

Shaking off her embarrassment, she headed up the steps to the porch, where five vacant rocking chairs swayed back and forth, as though each in tune with a separate melody.

The screen door creaked open and Cora appeared, wearing weathered jeans, a faded blue Western shirt and cowboy boots, her usual attire. "Laney? Laney Taylor? You're a sight for sore eyes." The door smacked shut behind her as she stepped outside.

Laney hurried into the older woman's arms and relished the warm embrace. She smelled of sugar cookies and soap. "Mrs. McCaw." This sweet woman had always provided patience and a listening ear when Laney craved guidance during her July stays. And she'd shown Laney what a true woman of God acted like.

"You're old enough to call me Cora." The heavyset woman pulled back and gazed at Laney with warm brown eyes. "I am heartbroken about Alice and Arthur. Such a tragedy."

"Thanks." The horrific head-on collision had killed Laney's aunt and uncle instantly. Though that knowledge didn't help as she grieved them. "I don't want to keep you, but I need to apologize for not speaking with you at the memorial service." She spoke around the lump forming in her throat.

"Oh, honey." She squeezed Laney's hands. "I'm so sorry you had to go through that." Cora looped her fingers through Laney's arm. "After that long drive, you must be tired. I just made a fresh pitcher of lemonade."

A few minutes later, they settled into the welcoming rockers, and Laney sipped the sweet, icy drink.

"I hear you're going to convert Alice and Arthur's ranch into a wedding venue." Cora set her rocking chair in motion. Laney did the same.

"Shabby-chic. Rustic. You know, what all the brides are looking for these days." Laney grinned, excitement swirling in her chest. "The beautiful old barn will hold the intimate receptions. We'll gut the interior to allow space for heavy farm tables. String twinkle lights all over for ambience." She could see it all, and more. Laney would call the shots and be in charge of her future and her life. Ever since her unstable childhood, she'd yearned for control. Now she'd have it in spades.

Laney hesitated. "Do you think Aunt Alice and Uncle Arthur would approve?"

"Oh, sweetie." Cora patted her hand. "I know they would. Alice had mentioned your plans to me before they passed."

Tears threatened, but she tamped them down. "At the memorial service, it hit me that I won't get to speak with my aunt and uncle again. Ever. That's why I ran out." She'd always assumed she'd have longer with them. Longer to work on her career. Longer to implement her dreams. Except that day she'd realized God's truth: He doesn't promise tomorrow.

"It was an emotional day for all of us, sweetie. No one took it personally. Certainly not me."

A warm breeze lifted the hairs around her

face, and she pushed them back. With Aunt Alice gone, the success of her new business had become even more important because she wanted her aunt to be proud of her.

Cora glanced at her watch.

Laney stopped rocking. She'd taken up enough of the older woman's time. "I don't want to keep you."

"I'm just concerned about Wade," Cora said. "A bull kicked him last week."

She straightened. "Oh, no. Is he okay?" Cora and Wade were like peanut butter and jelly. She never thought of one without the other. "Can I help in any way?"

"You are a darling to ask, but he'll be fine." She patted Laney's hand. "He has a concussion but he's on the road to recovery. A friend is inside with him right now, giving me a respite." She placed her dripping glass on the table. "Just give me a moment to check on him."

As Cora scurried inside, a new house beyond a swath of trees caught Laney's attention. An established weeping willow tree shaded the small, unassuming one-story home, and a warm white picket fence surrounded the property.

A contented sigh slipped past her lips. She'd always longed to live in a house like that. Similar to the one her childhood best friend had lived in. Had it been the inviting home or the family who lived there? She wasn't sure. But to Laney, a white picket fence equated a happy family.

Cora returned and sank into the rocker, visibly relieved. "He's napping." She nodded. "I got your email about a handyman and no one comes to mind, but I'll think about it."

"Thank you, Cora." To save money, her contractor would do the big jobs, and she planned to tackle the agreed-upon homeowner list. Except, since she wasn't handy at all, she was searching for just the right person to assist her. Guess she'd have to keep looking.

Laney heard squealing from the barn, and she turned. A muscular man pushed a jogging stroller carrying two little girls, one dressed in pink, the other in purple, down the hill toward them.

"That's our oldest, Ethan. You probably remember him from camp. He led the riding lessons."

Laney's breath caught. That was Ethan? The boy who had never let her help with anything? He'd probably thought his kid sister's friend an annoyance to shake off. But Laney had truly wanted to learn. She'd fantasized about being a cowgirl one day. Then she'd grown up.

In her teen years, Ethan had been friendly

in the riding ring, but elsewhere at the camp, he was always aloof. She wondered if anything had changed since they last saw each other.

He sported a blue-and-green-checked shirt, coupled with worn jeans, scuffed-up cowboy boots and the expected straw Stetson atop his head. Even from far away, his spicy cologne wafted over, intriguing her when she needed to remain solely focused.

The girls, who appeared to be identical twins, started an awkward clap. "Memaw, Memaw," they called, squirming from their strapped seats.

As he neared the porch, he offered a tired half smile. That was right—Aunt Alice had mentioned his wife had deserted him soon after the girls were born. She gave him a nod of encouragement. Being a single father must be exhausting.

He locked the stroller in place and unbuckled the girls. They were the most adorable children she'd ever seen. Not that she was into kids.

"What are my grandbabies up to today?" Cora opened her arms, and the girls rushed into them.

"We got eggs, Memaw," the one in pink stated. "They're in the fwidgewatow now."

"Girls, this is a friend of mine, Miss Laney."

Cora looked down at the twins. "This is Zoe—" she pointed to the one in pink "—and this is Tori. They just turned three."

"And their daddy, Ethan." As she gazed up at her son, Cora's face shone with love and respect.

He palmed off his dusty hat. "Sorry for your loss, Laney. Alice and Arthur were good folk." His burnt-almond eyes radiated warmth and sympathy.

Her vision started to blur as she shifted her focus to the toddlers.

White-blond ringlets framed the twins' tanned faces, the opposite of Ethan's dark brown hair. They must have inherited their mother's coloring.

Just then, a golden retriever raced onto the porch, its whole body wiggling as it stood in front of Ethan. "What's up, boy? Wanna play with the girls?" He scratched the dog's head, then hung his Stetson on a nail above the window.

Zoe and Tori scrambled off Cora's lap. "Bandit!" they shouted at the same time.

"Be gentle, girls," Ethan reminded them with tenderness.

While Bandit licked Tori's face, his exuberant writhing bumped Zoe, and she fell to the porch floor. Her face scrunched up, and she wailed. The dog danced around Tori.

Ethan rushed over to the girls. "Bandit, down." He swooped a crying Zoe into his arms as Bandit dropped to the ground, head between his paws. "It's okay, honey."

Laney thought she might swoon. A muscular, brawny man comforting his young child would do that to any woman, right? No! That was how her mother rolled, not Laney. She glanced away.

"Ethan, Laney plans to turn Arthur's place into a wedding venue."

He regarded Laney. "Arthur mentioned he willed you the land. We've been leasing most of it the last ten years for cattle grazing. I assume you'll continue to honor his contract?" His dark eyes sparkled, but no longer with warmth.

"I had no idea." She rubbed her forehead at the disturbing news. A land lease meant income. Money she could use for the renovation and her business as it grew, but sharing the land was not part of her plan.

"Yup. We have a signed contract and everything." His jaw twitched.

Her heart caught in her throat.

She'd given up her San Antonio life to start fresh in Serenity. Failure was not an option.

Willow Creek Ranch was huge. Surely there

was a way to negotiate some sort of compromise. "Maybe we can work something out?"

Her goal was to get her venue up and running. Though it would be awful if her business became a nightmare for the McCaws. Because these people—Cora especially—were the closest thing to a family she had left.

Maybe we can work something out?

Ethan McCaw's stomach dropped. Laney made it seem like she might not honor her uncle's lease. Like her plans for the property didn't include the McCaws.

He remembered Laney as his little sister's annoying friend who always wanted to help around the ranch. If only she'd be a little more helpful now.

Ethan shifted Zoe to his other arm. As she startled, then snuggled tight, he breathed in the baby smell mixed with active toddler.

"To be perfectly honest, we'd hoped to buy you out." When Arthur mentioned he was willing the ranch to Laney, Ethan assumed she wouldn't want the hassle of owning land hours away from her home in San Antonio. He looked to his mother for support, but her eyes were pressed closed. Most likely praying.

"Willow Creek Ranch is not for sale," Laney said, her voice full of indecision.

"We depend on that lease." If only he didn't sound as desperate as he felt, but he had to fight for his family. He paced across the wide porch as Zoe's sagging body radiated heat against his already warm arms. Somewhere along the way, she'd fallen fast asleep. "We've been leasing a good portion of Arthur's plot for a decade."

"Why?" With her eyebrows scrunched together, her prior disagreeable attitude seemed to blow away in the afternoon breeze.

"There's a high demand for 100 percent grass-fed cattle. When we switched to a daily pasture rotation, we needed more acreage." He leaned against the porch post. "Since Arthur had all but retired, we began leasing the southeast portion of his land. The solution worked well for both of us."

When Arthur offered to subdivide, they should have jumped at the chance to buy the property outright, but things hadn't sounded urgent. Writing Arthur a check every month seemed less painful than taking out a hefty mortgage. Now he wished they'd grasped the opportunity when it had presented itself.

Tori sat beside Bandit and petted his front

paws. His tongue lolled to the side as he leaned his head against the cool brick house.

"Ethan saved our family business with his newfangled suggestion. You know, that whole farm-to-table food everyone wants nowadays." His mother reached out and caressed Zoe's leg, dangling from his arms. "Admit it, kiddo—you rescued us. Our sales were dwindling until you came up with your genius idea."

He felt his cheeks heat from his mother's praise. "Sure, Mom."

The alarm on his mother's phone trilled, and she stood. "I have to give Dad his medication. Be right back." She scurried through the screen door.

"Do you use all the land?" Laney shifted to face him, her brows raised in question, like she genuinely cared.

He wasn't sure he remembered those mesmerizing aquamarine eyes from his childhood. They drew him in, awakening memories of her infectious laugh during bonfires, her careful and serious attitude around the horses, and her sweet gentleness with the younger campers. Maybe she hadn't *always* been a pest.

He cleared his throat. "We move the cattle daily, and we have a variety of grasses growing on Arthur's land." He rubbed his chin. "We put time and money into readying those pastures." Which meant if they found another plot elsewhere, they'd have to till and plant seed and also build more fencing. More time, more money and lots of inconvenience. A wedding place couldn't require much acreage, right?

His arm started to ache. Though Zoe wasn't big for her age, right now she felt like a cinder block.

"So, you're running the Triple C with your father?"

Tori stood and toddled to the steps.

"Stay up here, pumpkin." A glance at his watch startled him. Where had the time gone? He had to return to the barn, and if he wanted to accomplish anything this afternoon, the girls required a nap. Except he needed someone to watch the girls.

"Yes," he answered. "My mom handles everything with the youth camp. Dad and I manage the ranch."

"Up, up, Daddy." Tori reached out to him while Zoe slumbered in his arms.

Laney scooped up the child and cooed comforting words to her. Tori gazed at her and lifted a blond lock of Laney's naturally wavy hair, as though enthralled that it matched her own color.

"Thanks, but I can take her." He laid Zoe in

the play yard on the porch for this very reason, and smoothed her pink top. When he turned, Laney blew a soft breath on his daughter's face. Tori giggled.

He reached out and took his daughter from her. Strange, because out of his two children, Tori wasn't fond of strangers, yet she seemed more than fine with Laney. As he moved Tori to his hip, she stared at Laney. Laney closed her hands in front of her eyes, then opened them, a gigantic smile splayed across her rosy face. He couldn't get over the connection between Laney and Tori. Where had this consummate businesswoman learned how to play peekaboo with toddlers?

"She is so sweet."

Because of Dad's injury, his mother couldn't watch the girls at the usual time, dawn through lunch. And with the camp opening soon, she'd be busier than ever. If Dad couldn't be at the ranch, managing the place was up to Ethan.

He'd been searching for a summer sitter, but so far he'd found no one. This morning his mother had split a short list of additional possibilities between them.

Camp started Monday, the first of June, so he only had five days to fill the temporary nanny position. What if he didn't secure someone?

His stomach dropped. Their two cowhands, coupled with some neighbor ranchers, tried to fill Dad's shoes, but their efforts didn't cover the workload. For a cattle rancher, there was always something left undone.

The screen door slapped behind his mother. Tori squirmed down and scrambled over to her. His mother picked her up and settled in the rocker.

"How's Dad feeling today?"

"Still dizzy every time he moves."

So Pops wasn't able to watch the girls. But in five days, maybe…

"Oh, poor thing," Laney stated. "Do you mind if I go in and say hi?"

"He'd like that."

Laney went inside. She seemed to care for his mom and dad, but he worried about their agreement with Arthur.

"I took your dad to the doctor this morning. Based on his symptoms, the doctor expects him to be on the slower side of recovery." She spoke in soothing tones and rocked Tori, whose fussiness soon gave way to a well-deserved rest.

Earlier in the day, Ethan had contacted everyone on the list of nanny candidates his mother had given him. For a variety of reasons, none of the ladies could work for him. Thankfully, his mother had a couple of ladies she planned to reach out to.

"Did you have time to make your calls?"

"I did," she said. "I'm sorry—none of them can do it." His mother pulled a sad face, and the severity of the situation hit him like a raging bull.

He ran a hand through his unruly hair, ignoring his churning stomach. If Dad were healthy, it wouldn't be a big deal. But come Monday, Mom would be knee-deep in running the camp, and Ethan couldn't get on a horse and move the cows to another pasture with the twins in tow.

"Mom, what am I gonna do?"

While he paced up and down the porch, his mother tapped her index finger against her lips. Somehow he had officially run out of options.

Laney stepped onto the porch and held the screen door so it didn't creak as it closed. After she peeked at Zoe, she returned to the rocker.

"Oh, I have a great idea." His mother's sparkling eyes darted between him and Laney. "You need a nanny, and she needs someone to help with the renovation. How about the two of you work together and exchange services?"

"What? Aren't you hiring a contractor?" He remembered the headache of building his own house. "You can't do plumbing and electrical work on your own."

She shot him an I'm-not-an-idiot look. "I've hired a contractor for the big stuff, but I'd like to do as much as I can on my own. Demo, paint—you know, to save money." She twirled a blond lock and then released it. "I was actually looking to hire someone. Anyway, I'm not sure I'd have the time to watch the twins." She shifted in her seat, as though uncomfortable, her gaze dropping to the floorboards.

Good. Because he didn't have enough hours in the day to finish his own to-do list. And no matter how maternal Laney seemed, he was uncomfortable leaving the twins with a near stranger. How could Mom even suggest this?

His mother's friend Opal came out of the house. "Cora, he's still sleeping, but I have to get going."

"Thank you, sweetie." Mom hugged her friend. "Laney, I'm going to sit with Wade, but don't be a stranger." She laid Tori in the play yard next to her sister and slipped inside.

Laney stood and stretched her arms wide, as though tight from the long drive from San Antonio. She wore skinny jeans and a slim-fitting tee, coupled with a flimsy scarf that must be considered fashionable. Even dressed down, he could spot a city gal a mile away.

Ethan gazed at his sleeping girls. The only thing his mother had right was that he had to find someone to watch the twins for the next six weeks. The same amount of time left on the lease he hoped Laney would renew.

"They're beautiful," Laney whispered.

Those soft words wound around his heart, and whether he wanted to admit it, he needed Laney's help.

If he helped with her renovation project, then he'd know her plans for the leased land and how the Triple C could adjust.

"I can help with the demo and paint if you'd be willing to watch the twins for me."

Her smile flattened. "Oh, Ethan." She shook her head. "I just don't think I'll have time to watch your girls. I'm sorry."

He drew in a tight breath. Laney, though not a perfect choice, was his last option.

A vise tightened around his chest. What was he gonna do now?

Chapter Two

Ethan slipped his truck into Park and looked through his bug-plastered windshield at Alice and Arthur Taylor's—now Laney's—two-story farmhouse.

Yesterday Ethan thought his mother was absurd to suggest the bartering idea. Especially when he'd point-blank asked Laney to nanny the girls and she rejected him. But after she left, his mother reminded him that he needed to let people in instead of anticipating rejection.

That was when he'd realized that he and Laney helping each other was brilliant. Now, the trick was to convince her.

He unfolded his tall frame from his truck and stepped onto the gravel drive. The once-pristine siding appeared weatherworn, but the front porch still beckoned with comfy swivel chairs, as though Alice would invite him to sit with a glass of her amazing sweet tea.

Man, he'd miss the kindhearted couple. His heart ached for Laney, especially because the accident had been sudden, so she hadn't gotten a chance to say goodbye to them.

An ear-piercing revving noise filled the air. If the twins were here, they'd clap their little hands against their ears.

Arthur's beat-up UTV rounded the corner with Laney at the wheel. When she parked the vehicle next to the barn, the thundering sound halted. She threw him a welcoming smile, then replaced her rubber muck boots with little sneakers and headed his way.

They met in the center of the lawn.

A chorus of moos from the cattle in a nearby pasture lifted into the warm air. He contemplated how best to bring up the bartering idea.

"Aunt Alice and I—" Laney started.

"I came over—" They spoke at the same time. Ethan gestured with his hand. "Ladies first."

She blew a wheat-blond strand of hair away from her heart-shaped face. "I was going to say that Aunt Alice and I loved talking about creating a wedding venue and the renovations we would do to get the business up and running."

"Really? Because Arthur never mentioned it to me."

"I talked with my aunt on my commute to work every morning. Over the years, the talks shifted from my daily life to the practical changes we'd make for the remodel." Her voice wavered. "If I hadn't been so afraid of leaving my familiar life in San Antonio behind, I would have returned to Serenity while my aunt and uncle were still alive."

Her ocean-blue eyes filled with tears. Oh, no, was she going to cry?

He cleared his throat. "I get it. Tragedy strikes and then your life gets turned upside down. That's what happened when Joy, my ex-wife, left me and the babies."

Understanding and compassion flickered on her face. "I'm so sorry, Ethan."

In silence, he looked around the farm. The run-down barn snagged his attention. That was a far safer topic than his failed marriage. "After the accident, I brought Arthur's horses and chickens to the Triple C."

She lifted her palms. "You can keep them. I'm turning the barn into the reception hall."

"I take it you'll need me to move my hay also?" The longer their conversation went on, the more complications cropped up.

"That's your hay? I was wondering about that. It'll have to be cleared out, if you don't mind."

One more thing to add to his growing to-do list: find somewhere else to store his winter hay.

Ethan took a deep breath and said, "Remember what my mom suggested yesterday, about us trading services?"

She pulled an elastic band from her wrist and stuck it between her sparkling white teeth, then secured her wavy locks into a low ponytail. She didn't respond.

"You'd get weekends off. My mom is free then."

"Even though they are supercute and seem well-behaved, I'm not sure about caring for twins. I've watched a friend's toddler, but there was only one and I barely made it through the evenings. Kids are a lot of work. Two seems just about impossible." Laney began walking to the porch. "Let's get some shade. I'm not used to being out in the sun so much."

He rubbed the back of his neck and trailed after her. At least she thought the twins cute and well-mannered. That was a start. As he joined Laney on the wide front steps, he noticed her city-girl manicure, so out of place around here.

"Water?" She opened the screen door.

"No, thanks." He removed his cowboy hat and punched the center. A puff of dust sprayed out and landed on the dingy porch boards. He sank into one of the swivel chairs, wondering how to turn this conversation back to her babysitting the twins.

Laney returned with a water bottle. She pressed the half-full drink to her red cheeks and sank into a chair. "While I was out riding across the property, I narrowed down the spots for ceremonies. Aunt Alice and I had found dozens over the years, but today I selected my ten favorites. I tell you, I've fallen in love with this place all over again."

"Wait—I thought you were just renovating the house and the barn." His voice warbled with emotion. The Triple C relied on Arthur's land.

She cocked her head and blinked, as though confused. "Ethan, a wedding venue needs ceremony locations as well as space for the reception. They're a package deal." Her voice had softened. Presumably she'd realized the best choice for everyone was to work with him. "I want to find pretty locations here at Willow Creek Ranch for the exchange of marriage vows."

Her words seared the air between them. A pretty location? He hoped beyond hope she wouldn't pick the bluff overlooking the creek. It was on the edge of two fast-growing grass pastures they frequently used. He could only imagine the impact it would have on their cattle and grazing rotation.

"In fact, lots of venues have a variety of different backdrops on the property for the bride to choose from." She gazed into the distance.

His heart dropped. He had thought her signing was just a formality. What if she wouldn't renew their land contract before the lease ran out? Desperation choked him. Their success relied on the extra grazing pastures.

Sure, they had a contingency plan, but the other available acreage was miles down the road, which meant transporting cattle to that parcel and back.

"Maybe we could ride out on the UTV sometime?" he said. "Talk about the pros and cons of each location?" He hoped he could provide input to her plan. There had to be a win-win solution here.

"Oh, I was going to have a friend give me her opinion. I mean, she gets the whole wedding thing. But thanks anyway."

His shoulders slumped, but then he recalled the devotion he'd read this morning about not worrying about tomorrow, for tomorrow will worry about itself. He pushed his fear over the contract renewal aside and focused on the pressing issue of hiring a nanny. "You know, my girls are pretty easy to watch." He gulped at the broad generalization. *Usually* they behaved, but when left with a new person, they tested boundaries. Perhaps they'd be different with Laney? They'd spent time with her yesterday, so maybe they'd mind their manners.

"I hear you're the master of multitasking, so you might succeed at getting other work done at the same time." Maybe he could promise them a swim in Pops and Memaw's pool if they were on their best behavior. Yes, some considered it bribery, but as a single dad raising twins, it truly was a necessity.

"No, I can't watch them and do any remodeling. That would be impossible." She frowned.

"You're right." He was the first to admit that accomplishing anything while watching his girls was close to impossible, but sometimes he could do simple things like throw a meal together, put away dishes or do a load of laundry. They were precocious and adorable, but also curious and busy and, well, they got into trouble. A lot.

"I'm sorry, Ethan. It doesn't feel like a fair trade."

His chest tightened. She was right—he would get the better end of the bargain. The first day might be rough, but the girls *could* behave. And since he'd built his own house, he was knowledgeable about construction. And desperate, because she was his last resort for childcare. He had to change her mind, though she seemed determined not to watch his girls.

"I just don't understand why Arthur didn't tell me about your plans. You know, give me a heads-up." Arthur had never been a detail-oriented person. Could it be that he'd assumed Laney would only need the home and barn for her venue and that she'd continue to lease out the pastures?

At his words, her lips pressed together. "I don't think they planned on dying," she said as her sky blue eyes teared up. Again.

Regret constricted his throat. She was right. He still felt the ache of Arthur and Alice's loss.

He had come over to beg her to be a nanny to his girls and managed to upset the only person left in town who could help him.

Could this day get any worse?

Laney clapped a hand to her mouth. "Ignore me. That was the grief talking." The way Ethan's face shadowed reminded her that she wasn't the only one mourning.

Leaves from the enormous oak trees rustled in the breeze, breaking the awkward silence. "I'm not sure why Arthur said nothing to you, Ethan. He asked me ten years ago if I wanted the place, and I jumped at the chance."

For years, she'd worked nonstop as an event planner, like a hamster on an endless running wheel. She could kick herself for not visiting her aunt and uncle more frequently.

During their daily phone conversations, Aunt Alice had pressed her about when she'd come to Serenity to start her business. Her aunt had hoped to take part in the process, but fear had kept Laney rooted in San Antonio. Their sudden deaths had forced Laney to reconsider her goals. She couldn't change the past, which she deeply regretted, but she was here now. "My uncle knew my plans. I guess he never paid attention to the details?"

Ethan pinched his lips together. "I guess." The trilling of birdsong sounded in the distance, happy and carefree—the exact opposite of the way Ethan looked right now.

Learning of the McCaw lease had kept her tossing and turning all night. She'd thought the land was all hers. Part of her wanted the entire ranch for her venue, an expansive and peaceful space for each wedding party. The more responsible side knew Aunt Alice and Uncle Arthur would want her to come up with some reasonable arrangement and honor her uncle's obligation. With six weeks left on the lease, she had to come up with a way to share the property so they could work together.

With the late-afternoon sun sitting behind him, she shaded her eyes and met his gaze. "I can tell this is more than business to you, Ethan. Why is the lease so important?" The young boy who'd never let her help with anything had somehow turned into a broken man. As a youngster, his life had always appeared effortless. Today, a weight seemed to hang on each word Ethan spoke.

His ever-present Stetson shadowed his eyes, so she wasn't sure what he was thinking.

"I was fifteen when my grandfather died. I promised him I'd work with my dad to save the family ranch." As though restless, he stood and leaned against the pillar. "Our profits had been declining." He swallowed, then scrunched his face in worry. "A few years after Granddad passed, we switched to a daily pasture rotation to produce grass-fed cattle. I thought we had saved the Triple C."

He didn't say the words *until you showed up*, but he didn't have to. She had assumed the land was hers to do with as she pleased, and he had assumed she'd want to sell. They both needed to calm down, accept reality and work out some type of compromise.

"I get it. I've given up my career and plan to use all my savings, plus a hefty line of credit, to renovate." The stability of her prior life tugged, but she pushed it away. Her goal of success, and with it the autonomy she'd always longed for, was here for the taking. "Of course, the reason they left me Willow Creek is that, from an early age, I'd always set the table real pretty and gather wildflowers for the centerpieces. I made every event, even a simple dinner, special. And I loved to put on parties."

"I know you had an unstable home life as a kid." His eyes softened. If she didn't pay attention, she could get lost in those chocolate pools. "Your summer visits here were a respite from that life."

She felt her cheeks heat. "Your sister can't keep a secret." During Laney's childhood, her mother had relied on every man she met to take care of her—to take care of *them*. Her mother changed her personality to please each man and, in the process, lost her identity. That was why Laney would never have a relationship. Unlike her mother, she didn't need a man.

She gazed across the open fields. "For the past few years, every time I visited, my aunt and I would walk the property and make plans. I feel like the venue also became Aunt Alice's dream. No one ever believed in me the way she did. Now she's entrusted me with the ranch, and I can't let her down." Her vision blurring, she blinked.

He scraped a hand through his hair that drifted down the back of his neck, not quite touching his shoulders. "She was always so proud of you."

Arthur's golden retriever suddenly raced into the yard, barking. His appearance broke the tension and allowed her to clear her thoughts. She needed to live in the moment and leave the past behind.

As soon as Ace spotted them, he scrambled up the steps and ran straight to Ethan. As he sniffed the cowboy, the dog's entire body shook with excitement. Ethan leaned down to scratch the gentle dog's head, Ace's red-gold face now mostly white.

"He likes you." She drained her water bottle, confused about why the dog ignored her.

The golden retriever lifted his nose and

sniffed around Ethan's pockets. All Laney could smell was the man's spicy scent.

"He's looking for food." Ethan grinned.

"I fed him this morning." Understanding dawned. "You've been coming over to feed him?" Her voice lifted at the end.

"He won't leave the property." Ethan chuckled. "I drove him to our place after we heard the news, but he came back here." He rubbed Ace's ears. "I've been dropping in daily to fill his food and water dish."

"For two months? That's so…generous," she said. "I don't even know my neighbors in San Antonio. I mean, I pass them in the hall and mumble a greeting, but I don't know their names."

"It's no big deal. Cities are different than small towns."

His words made her long for the community of Serenity to make her feel like part of a family.

She gazed over the sheared lawn. "I take it you mowed?" When she'd arrived yesterday and stepped out of her car, the pungent smell of fresh-cut grass had hit her.

"I've been mowing every few weeks to stave off ticks and snakes, you know?" He glanced over at Ace.

This guy was the real deal. She didn't like where her thoughts were traveling. She hopped out of her chair. "Let me show you what I plan to tackle."

In the kitchen, he removed his Stetson, and she pointed. "The wall between the dining and living room is coming down, and that space will turn into the groomsmen's lounge, with club chairs and a couple of wall-mounted televisions. I'll refinish the hardwoods on the first floor." She tossed her water bottle into the garbage and reached for the cool garage doorknob.

"Wait. A contractor will take down the wall, or at least make sure it isn't load-bearing, right? And fill in the hardwood? And any electrical work?" He slid his hat onto the peeling laminate.

"Of course. I'll focus on the simpler things, to save money." She rubbed her arms, the desire to flee overwhelming her. Had she agreed to too much responsibility in this remodel? *Maybe.* "I have a good friend in San Antonio who is also a financial planner. After I narrowed down the quotes and selected a contractor, Rose and I came up with a strategy that I plan to stick with."

Last night on the phone, Rose had encouraged her to trade services with Ethan. Reminded Laney that relying on someone didn't make you weak and vulnerable. *You will not lose control of the project by having someone who knows about construction helping you. You are not your mother.*

Rose was so wise. Except control wasn't the issue. What troubled her was the prospect of dealing with a pair of active twin toddlers.

She stepped into the empty two-car garage. "This will turn into a bride's dressing room, adorned with chairs and mirrors for makeup and hair, comfy couches for attendants and family to relax on, and a huge mirror for the bride to see how gorgeous she looks on her special day." She couldn't wait for it all to become a reality.

"So, the contractor will lay the floor? And do all the electrical and plumbing?" he asked, his eyebrows drawing together.

"Yup." She lifted onto her toes and surveyed the area. "Obviously, this will become a solid wall, with some windows for light." She gestured at the aluminum garage door.

"What jobs are *you* planning to do?"

They moved back into the house, and she leaned against the kitchen counter. She reminded herself of the reason for his visit—he wanted to trade services. Maybe tempering her excitement with his realism would be a smart move. "Painting the house, barn and kitchen cabinets. Removing the wallpaper." She ticked the items off with her fingers as she listed them. "Refinishing the hardwoods. Replacing all the light fixtures. Cleaning out the interior of the barn. Those sorts of things."

The list sounded endless and impossible, but she'd rather hire someone than work side by side with Ethan. If she employed someone, paid them a salary, she was the boss.

He nodded. "The house needs a good power wash before you paint." He looked around the space, and his gaze snagged on her. "I built my house, you know. I could help you. I mean, if you'd reconsider and watch Tori and Zoe for me."

No way was Laney going to watch a pair of three-year-olds, even if they were adorable. Except, after all he'd done for her aunt and uncle, and now Ace and the lawn mowing… Maybe she owed him? She nibbled her lower lip. "You've got to have other childcare options than me."

He shook his head. "So many people work at the camp this time of year. Every other person I or my mother know isn't available to help. You're kind of my last hope."

"But we barely know each other," she countered.

"You were honest and smart as a kid, and yesterday you interacted with them like a pro. I think you'd do a fine job watching my girls."

The world tilted at the confidence behind his words. Her cheeks flamed. He remembered her. Four years younger than him, she'd never thought he'd known she existed.

Then her gaze caught on the massive to-do list tacked to the refrigerator she'd promised her contractor she'd handle. What had she been thinking? Her huge renovation merited some skilled help, because if she were honest, without YouTube, she was completely clueless. But there was something to be said about completing all the tasks on her list without falling into any more debt than the current construction loan. And though she didn't want to add nannying to her plate, Cora would appreciate it. "How much will you be able to help me if you have a ranch to run?"

He slid his Stetson back onto his head. "I was thinking you could watch them from dawn until eleven. Your aunt watched them here from time to time." He shrugged. "Unless you want to come over to my place?"

"Here would be superconvenient."

"Okay. My mother will watch them later in the afternoons, so I can help you most days, say, from three to six? I'll do whatever you tell me to do." He moved to the porch and held open the door for her.

They both needed help. It was a simple exchange of services. Taking care of his sweet girls would not put her independence in peril. She stepped through the door, he released his hold and it smacked shut.

After all he'd done, out of the goodness of his own heart, maybe she should truly consider his idea. "Okay, let's give this a try."

"Can you start Monday? I hope you're an early riser."

"I am."

"Great. I'll drop them off at five thirty."

She gasped.

"Too early?"

"Well, it's kind of the middle of the night. But I guess on a ranch…"

"Okay, well, I can push it to a bit after six, if that's more palatable for you. The girls will still be asleep and in their pajamas." He gave her a charming smile, thanked her and drove away, dust flying up behind his truck.

A sinking feeling clawed at her gut. She had just committed to babysitting twins.

Her. A professional event planner.

She could handle a hysterical bride or a demanding mother of the groom. A last-minute floral change or a missing tuxedo? No problem.

But a pair of mischievous toddlers? Her hands trembled at the thought of Monday morning.

Yet she knew if she wanted her wedding venue to become reality, she required someone's help. And Ethan had built his own house. She needed him.

Chapter Three

Musicians sat on the platform in Serenity's town square tuning their instruments. Ethan tapped his fingers against his jeans, trying to ignore Laney, who sat next to his mother, fidgeting. Maybe she thought this event was hokey. Joy certainly had.

Most Friday nights, listening to the band in his tiny hometown invigorated him, but not tonight. He was still reeling from the possibility that Laney might not extend their land lease, even when she'd be receiving monthly payments to help with her wedding business. His chest tightened at the absurd notion that she didn't seem to think they could share the property. How much land could a wedding venue require?

"Has Austin texted you?" his mother asked.

"He and Eli should have been here by now." Her gaze roamed the crowds for his brother and Austin's two-year-old son.

Ethan's mother and father sat in navy camp chairs, exactly like they did on every other Pops in the Park night. The music and food might change weekly, but his steadfast parents never missed an opportunity to participate in family time.

"They aren't coming tonight. Neither is Carter."

Her smile wavered for a moment, but then returned. "You should show Laney around the center green." His mother indicated the brick path that ran around the green as she squeezed Laney's hand. "It's been a while since she's been here."

His brain scrambled for an excuse. Tori and Zoe sat on the family quilt spread out in front of his parents. The twins searched the crowd for their church friends. "I'm with them, remember?" He nodded in their direction, hoping she'd take the hint.

"Ethan, Laney is our guest. I'll keep an eye on the girls for you." His mother's sweet voice had that hard edge to it, a tone only family members could recognize.

He pulled his collar away from his neck.

"Sure. Okay." His parents had done so much for him. Their love and actions had motivated him to keep the promise he had made to his grandfather.

He planted a quick kiss on his mother's soft cheek, wishing this vulnerable feeling didn't swallow him up sometimes. When the whole family gathered, occasionally he felt disconnected from them. Like he didn't belong. Like he wasn't a true McCaw.

After he had a quick word with Tori and Zoe, he caught Laney's eye. "Want to walk around?" He wiped his sweaty hands on his pants. Why was he nervous?

"Sure." She released a lock of shoulder-length hair she'd been twisting.

They made their way over to the brick path that circled the town green. Random chatter and laughter filled the air.

"I thought you'd be a little mad at me." Laney's voice was so soft he almost didn't hear.

Her hesitation reminded him that he had to walk a fine line. Yes, she planned to start a business on the property they used, and their lease was up in the air. But she had also agreed to be his nanny. And he desperately needed childcare for the next six weeks.

"Of course I'm disappointed. But I hope we can come up with a compromise."

"I have to consider what's best for me in the long run." Her tone was firm.

"But—"

She stopped and extended her palm. "Ethan, I don't want to talk business tonight."

"Of course."

As she gazed around the square, a satisfied smile bloomed on her face. "I remember this event from childhood, and I just want to take it all in." She craned her neck, as though trying to see above the crowd. "Is that fried dough?"

"Yup."

She made a noise of longing.

He chuckled. "How about we get some?" Brownie points for Laney that she cared so much for the town he cherished. He headed toward the fried-dough food truck and ordered, but when he reached for his wallet, it wasn't there. Frantic, he patted all his pockets, though he always stowed his billfold in his right rear jeans pocket.

"I've got this." Laney slid a twenty across the counter.

Annoyed at his forgetfulness, he shoved his hands into his empty pockets and stepped away so she could pay.

As she turned toward him with a paper plate laden with fried dough covered in powdered sugar, her wavy hair lifted in the light breeze.

They settled on a park bench nearby. Ethan couldn't help but worry about how he could have forgotten his wallet. It was probably hidden in the towering stack of mail by the front door at home. At least he hoped it was.

She pointed. "Those food trucks are a great addition. Snow cones, sausages, tacos. A little bit of everything," she said between bites.

"Yes, and our local shops, What's the Scoop, Eatalian Pizza and Morning Grind, are also open." He popped a piece of dough into his mouth from the section she had shared with him.

She swallowed the last sweet bite. "Boy, that was good." She brushed the powdered sugar off her fingertips and stood.

He got up, and they continued to follow the brick path through the town square.

"This is perfect. Not too packed, but a nice-size crowd," she mused.

Ethan couldn't help but notice how much his little sister's friend had grown into a beautiful young woman. It was still hard for him to comprehend, because she and Autumn had always been such tomboys.

His phone dinged. Joy, his ex-wife, had texted. Hey, how are the kids? Hug and heart emojis ended the short message. If she truly cared, she'd be here with them. Instead, she sent him a text most Friday nights asking after the girls. Like a weekly check-in and nothing more. He shoved his phone back in his pocket, not texting her back.

Joy had been a city girl when he met her. During their whirlwind romance, she'd seemed to love him. But after their wedding vows, Joy had soon shown her true colors—she was self-ish, self-centered, disappointed with her pregnancy and completely uninterested in the twins once they'd been born. When Tori and Zoe turned two months old, she'd left them to return to her city life in Dallas.

"This place is wonderful, isn't it?" Laney pulled out her phone and snapped a couple of pictures.

He pushed thoughts of Joy from his mind and glanced overhead to where string lights ran from one side of the green to the other.

"You okay?" She tilted her head to look at him.

"Um, sure." He would not share how Joy had charmed him. He hadn't seen her true self until right before she'd left. Nope, not going there.

"Oh, there's First Church." Laney bounced on her toes like an excited kid. "Your mom told me that's where you all go. She said I could join her on Sunday."

Well, that was a plus. He was leaving his daughters with a woman of faith.

He looked across the bustling town square at his church and scrubbed a hand over his face. As a busy single parent, he'd gotten out of the habit of daily quiet time, which was not only hurting him, but his girls. How could he be a good father if he wasn't allowing God to guide him?

"Hey, Ethan." He whirled around at his sister's voice. "Who's your *friend*?" Autumn emphasized the last word.

He cleared his throat. "You remember Laney Taylor?"

She squealed. Laney squealed. Then they hugged, saying things about not keeping in touch and how they wouldn't make that mistake in the future. When they finally calmed down, they exchanged phone numbers.

For his sister to think he and Laney were together—well, he wasn't sure what she was thinking. She knew that after Joy, he was bound and determined against getting involved with another woman.

"Congratulations. I hear you're starting up a destination wedding venue." Autumn beamed.

"I'm so excited."

His sister took Laney's hands. "You used to be an event planner, right?" Autumn charged ahead. "My parents' anniversary is in a little over a month. I was wondering if you could plan a big surprise party for them?"

"Absolutely. I'd be honored."

"I'll text you, and we can coordinate." They hugged goodbye, and Autumn walked away.

As he and Laney continued their stroll around the town green, he made sure not to get too close. He didn't want anyone else to think they were an item. Small towns and all.

She pointed at the neat row of downtown shops. "Does Otto still run What's the Scoop? Do Agnes and Theo still own Morning Grind? Is Earl currently the veterinarian?" Each time he nodded, she grinned larger. "I can't wait to catch up with each of them, especially Earl."

He remembered how much she'd longed to be a veterinarian, like Earl, when she grew up. What had happened to her dream? He knew about her mother, but she'd had Arthur and Alice to lean on.

"Did you like living in San Antonio?"

She gazed into the distance. "Oh, yes. The

River Walk was my favorite. So many of our wedding venues were located along it, and our offices were only a block away."

Clearly, she was a city gal to her core. Independent. Resourceful. Ambitious. What would happen if his twins connected with her and then she returned to San Antonio? Would they feel rejected again?

A serious expression clouded her face. "You know, I used to call Aunt Alice and Uncle Arthur every morning on my way to work. Now I can never call them again." A tear trickled down her cheek.

"I'm so sorry." Her vulnerability drew him in. But he had to keep his mind on the goal: to renew the lease.

She stepped away and shook her head. "I can't believe the loss still hits me so hard after two months." She tried to smile, but it didn't quite reach her eyes. As she began strolling again, he joined her.

She'd said she didn't want to discuss business, but he simply had to know the status of their lease. The past few days, the uncertainty had been gnawing at him. Surely by now she'd made a decision.

"You know, I think you might be making too much of sharing the land. I mean, we could eas-

ily work around a ceremony location or two."
He stopped to let her step around a group of
ladies chatting. "I could give you the name of
a lawyer if you'd like to extend our lease."

She stopped and cocked her head. "I'm sorry,
Ethan. A wedding venue is so much more than
a building and a couple of backdrops." She
stared out into the distance, a faraway look in
her eyes. "I'll need some type of paved walkway for the guests to walk to the ceremony
sites. Maybe several." She shrugged.

He worked his jaw back and forth. They
could work through this. He would guide her
to areas of the land he didn't use regularly. This
could still work. He knew it.

"You know where the bluff is, at the end of
those really green fields?"

He sucked in a breath. "Yes. Those are our
fastest-growing pastures. We rotate in and out
of those two regularly."

"They're so pretty. So green and lush. That's
where I want the winding walkway. Right in
the center of those fields, with pretty twinkle
lights above."

"What?" His eyes bugged out. "You've got
to be kidding me. That'll run straight through
the pastures."

"Sorry, Ethan, but my venue comes first."

He rubbed the back of his neck. The hope of renewing their lease seemed to decrease as each day passed.

Somehow, he had to help her see that their two businesses could share the land.

But how?

"I would rather not talk business tonight." She needed time to think about the wedding venue, and him pushing her made her uneasy. It was difficult enough moving forward after discovering the McCaws were leasing some of the land she had her eye on for ceremony and photo shoot locations.

How could she lighten the mood?

"How about you?" she asked. "Are you glad you never left Serenity?"

Without his cowboy hat, Ethan's thick chocolate waves drifted down the back of his neck. If he were a businessman, he would need a trim. But since he was a cowboy, the longer locks looked just right.

"I love it here," Ethan responded, his tone light. "Couldn't imagine being anywhere else other than helping Dad run the Triple C."

It didn't escape her that the success of his ranch depended on her land. Hopefully the Mc-

Caws had an alternate plan, but surely nothing was as convenient as the property next door.

As dusk hit, they strolled across the street. The lampposts stood tall, wrapped in clear twinkle lights. The lower the sun moved, the more magical the town square appeared. Music from the concert sounded from the large gazebo.

"It was good to see Autumn. I can't believe we lost touch." It strengthened her confidence when her friend had asked her to plan a surprise party for Cora and Wade.

Even though Laney was self-sufficient and knew she could build this new business, she'd been flailing around in her head these past few days. Probably because of her overwhelming to-do list. And the contractor's price was only affordable based on the aggressive amount of work she had promised to do. But what if she wasn't able to pull it off?

Not having an income during this remodel had been worrying her. Which was why she had reached out to peers and already had one side job, to create a website, lined up.

"Seemed like you were best friends in your teens." He wiped his hands on his like-new jeans. A white-and-black-checked shirt stretched across his muscular chest. Almost like he dressed up for these events.

"We were." It was amusing to think Autumn believed Laney was dating Ethan. What would have given her that notion?

People milled about, talking with friends, ducking into shops and laughing with others. During her childhood, Serenity had been her happy place—at least every July. The month her mother got rid of Laney, freed herself from all adult responsibilities and sent her to Aunt Alice and Uncle Arthur.

People gathered in front of Morning Grind. Ethan led the way, guiding her through the crowd. His muscular shoulders created a wide berth for her. Applause from the concert lifted into the air.

"There's Earl." Ethan took off after the older man.

She rushed along behind him, excited to reconnect with her old friend.

"Earl," Ethan called out.

The veterinarian turned around. His features were the same as they'd been ten years ago, except with a few more wrinkles on his face.

"Laney." He opened his arms to hug her, smelling of hay and the wild outdoors.

The last week of summer camp, they had a presenter every day. Most kids went crazy for the fire truck, but not her. The veterinarian was her favorite. Because of him, she'd wanted to become a vet, but then she learned you had to go to college. And after her mother had ruined her credit, Laney was petrified of debt. Instead, she'd hired on full-time with the event-planning company she'd worked for during high school.

She was touched Earl remembered her from so long ago. Earl and the other welcoming people of this town made her feel like she'd come home.

After giving him a brief rundown of the renovation and her new business, she asked about him and his family.

"We're good, real good." He rested his hands on his wide midriff. "I'll tell you, Ace sure gave me a scare with that snakebite last month."

"What?" She flipped her attention between Ethan and the veterinarian. Her heartbeat raced at the thought of Arthur's sweet golden retriever being hurt.

"Oh, I'm sorry." The vet glanced at Ethan. "I assumed you knew."

"I didn't want to worry you," Ethan said. "About a month ago, when I arrived to feed Ace, I saw a dead copperhead near the house. It looked like maybe Ace had tangled with it. Then I found him on the porch, panting really hard and his neck swollen like a bullfrog's."

A copperhead. Oh, my. Her thoughts swirled so quickly she could barely follow Ethan's words.

"So, I brought him to Earl, who fixed him up."

She threw her hand over her chest. "Thank you, Dr. Earl. I really appreciate it." Tears formed in her eyes. "I don't know what I would have done if I'd come back and Ace wasn't around."

Earl nodded. "You're welcome. But the big thanks go to Ethan, who arrived in time. Snakebites are very painful and can be deadly. We started Ace on fluids and pain medication. Within three days, he was ready to go home."

"Yup. When I brought Ace to my parents' house after the stay with Dr. Earl, he went into the corner where my mom had made him a bed and slept for a couple of days. No energy. No appetite. And he stayed with us for almost a week before he headed back to Arthur's." Ethan chuckled.

Laney threw her arms around Ethan. "You're a hero." As soon as her arms reached around his neck, she realized her mistake and jumped back. Embarrassed, she stepped away. "Thanks again. I still can't believe you've been driving over to feed him every day. And mowing the lawn."

And here she was, unwilling to share the land with him. No. She bit her tongue before she could say anything she'd regret. She refused to allow the good deed of saving Ace's life to change her mind about signing the contract.

As Earl walked away, she turned to Ethan. "Thank you." She lifted her chin, refusing to allow emotions in again. "Just text me the invoice. I'll reimburse you."

He shook his head. "No worries. Earl gave me a deep discount because Ace wasn't mine."

Only in a small town would a businessperson cut a deal with you because of extenuating circumstances. Her heart hiccuped. She couldn't believe she now got to call this place home. "That's very nice of him. But I don't like to be indebted. To anyone." Especially a handsome cowboy.

"Okay, I'll dig out the invoice and text it to you." He raked his fingers through his hair. "Let's get back to my folks and the girls."

She followed him through the growing crowd. When they arrived back at the McCaw quilt, Autumn was sitting with the girls, playing. Ethan's brother Walker rested in a camp chair, his cell phone to his ear. Cora and Wade flanked the blanket, tapping their toes to the music and holding hands like teenagers. Cora leaned her head on Wade's shoulder, and he whispered something in her ear. She beamed at her husband.

Because of her past, Laney believed she could never have a successful romantic relationship, so it was wonderful to see proof that marriages could work.

The minute the girls spotted their dad, they climbed up on him like a jungle gym.

Tori squealed as Ethan tipped her upside down, her curly blond hair cascading almost to the ground. His rumble of laughter filled the air.

Laney focused on the band instead of the captivating man in front of her.

For months, Ethan had come over to Willow Creek Ranch every day to feed Ace.

And mow the lawn.

And saved Ace's life.

He flashed her a smile. "They won't be this wild on Monday. I promise." He winked.

Monday. Who was she kidding? She was a control freak who knew little to nothing about construction and even less about watching kids. Especially twins.

She settled next to Autumn on the blanket and tried to ignore how her pulse pounded every time Ethan was near.

Maybe accepting his help wasn't the wisest

move on her part. Discovering Ethan had saved Ace and paid his vet bill made her indebted to him. If that was difficult for her to handle, how would doing renovation with Ethan work?

"I hear you and my brother are going to be helping each other."

The gravity of her financial situation sank in as Laney raised a shaky hand and tucked a wayward strand of hair behind her ear. "I guess so."

"What's wrong?"

"I know party planning, and a bit about website design and social media, Autumn. I should be hawking those services to make enough money to pay my contractor to do the overwhelming tasks on my list. Not babysitting in exchange for Ethan helping me." She fidgeted with her fingers. "What if we can't get stuff done in time for my contractor to start work?" Maybe more importantly, what if she was a horrible babysitter?

Autumn dismissed her with a wave of her hand. "Don't worry about it. Ethan built his house. He knows tons about construction."

She groaned. That was exactly the problem. He'd take over.

But she didn't have a choice. He needed a babysitter and she'd given her word.

Exchanging services for the next six weeks might have been the worst decision she'd ever made.

Except, it was impossible to back out now.

Chapter Four

Water gushed from the ceiling like Niagara Falls. Inches of water soaked the hardwood and the couch—and, well, everything.

Laney's lips quivered as she squeezed the towel over Aunt Alice's kitchen sink and rushed back. Between steps, water sloshed under her feet as she tried to salvage the hardwood. The upholstered furniture was a total loss.

She willed herself not to cry.

Where was the plumber? Her contractor had promised he'd send him immediately to turn off the water.

She saturated another towel and squeezed it over the sink. Scanning the scene, she pushed forward, doing the only thing she could think of: remove the water as best she could. But how much would this set back her construction project? Her budget?

"Laney, you here?" The screen door squeaked open, then clapped shut.

Ethan? *Thank You, Lord.* "Living room." A trickle of perspiration dripped into her eyes. She swiped it away with her forearm.

"Oh, no," he exclaimed. "Busted pipe. I'll turn off the water." He ran out of the house.

A few moments later, the waterfall dwindled to a few drops.

Yay! She blew a strand of hair off her damp face, thankful for the end of the deluge.

Ethan returned and dropped his worn Stetson on the peeling laminate counter. He gazed around the wet space, standing water still in the living room. The area she had hoped to convert into the groomsmen's lodge.

"Do you have a broom? A mop? Buckets?"

Nodding, she scrambled around, gathering them, grateful for his help.

He propped open the screen door and started sweeping water onto the porch with the stiff-bristled broom.

"Wait—that'll ruin the porch boards, won't it?" Her chest tightened at the sight of water in one more place. "It's bad enough the hardwood floors might be a complete loss." Her voice wavered.

He kept sweeping. "The porch is pressure-treated wood. It can withstand the water."

"Oh, okay. And thanks for making it stop raining in here." She moved to the living room and swished the mop around. It drank up water like a thirsty dog on a hot summer day. She pulled up on the trigger and squeezed out the water, almost filling a bucket in one load. Why hadn't she thought of a mop or broom earlier?

"No problem. Just turned off the water main valve at the street."

Now that the flood had ended, she took in the massive amount of water puddling on the floor. Her eyes misted. "What am I gonna do? I planned to refinish these and…" She couldn't think straight. It was only day four, and already her renovation plan and budget were a disaster. Kind of like these hardwoods. Her chin trembled.

"The faster we work and get the water off the wood, the better your chance of saving them." He moved past her and became more aggressive with his sweeping.

She put her head down and focused on mopping as quickly as possible. Here she'd been concerned he'd take over and he had. But with the burst pipe and water gushing out of the ceiling, someone had to take charge. Her stomach churned at her inexperience with everything home-improvement related.

After what felt like forever, the hardwoods were clear of standing water. Oh, they were still wet. And the finish seemed to be peeling right off.

"They're ruined." Her sore shoulders started to sag.

"I'm not gonna lie, they look pretty bad, but let's wait to see if they buckle."

Right. How much would new hardwood cost? Or maybe laminate that looked like hardwood? Either way, money she hadn't prepared to spend. Tears threatened.

"I laid hardwood floors in my house, so if it comes to that…"

She shook her head. She was already imposing too much. "We'll see."

He clapped his hands together. "Okay. Just so you know, you don't have water until the plumber has time to come out and fix the leak."

Ugh. No shower, no bathroom, no water in the faucets. She pressed her eyes closed. "Well, thanks for acting so quickly and turning it off. And for the broom and mop ideas." Somehow, she'd make it work.

"My pleasure." His T-shirt, splattered with water, hugged his impressive upper-arm muscles.

"The twins are eating lunch at my mother's and then taking their nap there. So I had a couple of hours free and thought you could use another set of hands."

Her cheeks heated that he'd chosen to help her. She hadn't expected him until Monday. All her negativity from last night flew into her head. Surely she and Ethan could work together—they'd just proved it, right?

She tried to put the plumbing debacle behind her so they could be productive today. "I appreciate it."

Watching the twins had seemed like the raw end of the deal, but with this plumbing problem and her lengthy to-do list, she was thrilled to have his help and support. She sucked in a calming breath.

Ethan nodded. "Today I thought we could power wash the house. I brought the pressure washer my dad and I purchased a few years back."

She applauded—anything to avoid staring at the peeling hardwood floors that were bound to warp and need replacing. "That sounds great." She pointed to the refrigerator. "It's on my to-do list." Something about Ethan soothed her nerves. Made her feel like she *could* handle her to-do list, and in a timely manner. The problem was, she needed him. And she disliked depending on other people. For anything.

"How are we going to power wash without water?"

"The old well is connected to the barn, so we should be fine." His deep voice filled the kitchen. They stepped outside, he hooked the equipment up and they both donned protective eyewear.

Ace danced around them and dropped a tennis ball at their feet. Laney kicked it away from the job site.

Ethan began washing the house. The simple back-and-forth movement with the wand looked easy. But it was a slow-going project. Very slow. Worry bubbled in her gut. Was this morning a sign of things to come?

She grabbed a rag and went behind him, drying the windows. Ace nuzzled under her hand, and she patted his head in between windows, thankful for his peaceful disposition.

Was she crazy to want to renovate her aunt and uncle's ranch for this purpose? After dreaming about opening her own wedding venue her entire adult life, she now owned the land to do it. Except, every little decision now loomed large and unattainable in her mind.

What if she failed? What if more horrible

things—like a pipe bursting and flooding the house—kept happening? That would be akin to letting her aunt down. And she didn't want that. Her mind traveled to Monday morning and the daunting task of caring for the twins.

"Do the girls get to see their mother often?"

"No. Joy left when they were babies and has limited contact with them. So they barely know her." Grief and regret mingled on his face.

Her ribs grew tight at the pain Joy had caused him. Laney's childhood crush may have caused her to pay a bit more attention to him than she should have in their younger years. That was probably the reason she felt so bad for the demise of his marriage.

Would Joy ever realize her mistake and want a second chance with them? With Ethan?

When he turned the power-washing machine off, country silence enveloped her. The birds tweeted; a lone cow mooed. Kind of peaceful, except her wooden floors were probably buckling at this very moment.

He tugged the contraption around the corner to tackle the other side of the house. "You mentioned Alice wanted you to come back to start your business for years. Why now?"

"I guess all these years it's been easier to stay in San Antonio. Aunt Alice kept encouraging me to come and start the business earlier, but I didn't have the guts." Each year, she'd seriously think about it. But then days would turn into weeks, and weeks into years.

"I'm happy for you, finally doing it. My father has been great guiding me with the ranch." He started the machine and continued the washing.

She focused on his last comment. About his father, encouraging him like her aunt had done for her.

Even though she and her mother had never seen eye to eye, she'd cherished her aunt and uncle and the influence they'd had in her life. As she grew older and realized she wasn't as wise as she once believed, she'd ended up talking with Aunt Alice every single day. She'd spent the past ten years soaking up life lessons from her aunt and uncle.

She gazed across Ethan's pastures and spotted a cow lumbering across her green yard, heading toward them. Her eyes widened. "What in the world?"

How were they supposed to share the land if his animals didn't stay in their space? The last thing she wanted was a cow to wander into a wedding ceremony or reception.

Her pulse pounded in her ears.

The McCaws had done so much for her, and her aunt and uncle, that Laney yearned for them to succeed.

Could she honor her uncle's lease, or would Laney's dream business ruin the Triple C Ranch?

As the bull neared him, Ethan reached his palm toward the Angus. His scratchy tongue felt like coarse sandpaper rubbing across his hand.

"Cows are the landscape of Texas." He tossed Laney a side glance. "No one will bat an eye if a cow wanders into a reception." Why was she making such a big deal over one cow getting loose?

She crossed her arms in front of her and scowled at the cow.

He scraped a nervous hand through his hair. Surely she wouldn't let a simple thing such as one loose cow persuade her not to renew their lease?

"They'd do way more than bat an eye," she snapped. "They'd expect a refund."

Uh-oh. She was upset.

Hackles up, Ace ran up to the cow and barked once, then stalked to his raised bed on the porch as though disgusted by the beast.

One of his ranch hands, Colt, rode up on his

horse. "Ma'am." He tilted his Stetson at Laney, then focused on Ethan. "Sorry about that, boss. This one got away as we were moving the herd." He shook some grain at the cow, who mooed and then trailed after the ranch hand.

"Thanks, Colt."

"You're welcome. Sorry about your flowers, ma'am," he threw over his shoulder.

Laney sucked in a breath and rushed to a mound of messy dirt by the porch. "Your cow ate my petunias!" Her pitch matched Zoe's when her twin stole one of her toys.

At her shriek, he strolled over and gazed at the barren space. "Sorry about that." The animal had probably smelled them this morning and made a mental plan of escape. He chuckled. No, cows weren't that smart—the getaway was likely an accident rather than a premeditated outbreak.

She glared at him, soulful aquamarine eyes narrowing. "This is funny to you? I spent an hour planting them last night." She clenched her hands at her sides.

Her floral fragrance lifted between them, halting his steps and mind.

A ding sounded from his phone. He pulled it out and swiped up. It was Joy. He didn't have the bandwidth to deal with his ex-wife right now. He shoved the device back in his pocket, Laney's frown catching his attention. "I'm sorry about your flowers. I'll reimburse you—just let me know how much they cost."

"It's more than the flowers. That cow…" She pointed at the Angus following Colt like a puppy and scrunched her nose. "That cow is the problem." She shot him a look he feared meant sharing the property might not happen.

Would she be unwilling to extend the lease just because a cow got loose every once in a while?

She tucked an errant lock of wavy hair behind her ear, her fortitude restored. "I'll take over the power washing." She stuck her goggles back on, then strode over to the machine, grabbed the wand and turned it on. The pink tool belt that lay at her waist shook with the motion of the work.

The fierce determination on her face spoke to her urgency to be in control. He stepped back and made a mental note not to take over projects. Everyone had issues—he was no different—but since she liked to be in charge, he'd tread carefully.

Soon her arms seemed to grow fatigued. She handed over the wand, a visible tightness in her jaw, and moved a few steps away.

"Great job," he encouraged her, trying to pacify her after the cow-escaping-and-eating-the-flowers ordeal. "The house is looking good." He picked up where she had left off, careful with his words and actions lest she feel like he was taking charge.

"It is. Thank you." Her words lifted over the machine's noise. She gave the place an appreciative appraisal. "Is your mom okay watching the twins and your father at the same time?"

Good. A topic other than wandering cows and eaten flowers. "Yup. He's not as dizzy as he used to be, so he can go to the bedroom and get some quiet when he tires out."

"Glad to hear that."

"I'm so grateful for my parents and siblings, who love and adore Tori and Zoe. You know Mom and Dad adopted me, right?" *Oh, my.* Could he not keep his mouth closed? Maybe she hadn't heard over the noise of the machine.

She spun around at his pronouncement, features displaying shock.

"I found out in middle school. Until then, I just assumed they were my biological parents."

"I had no idea." Her big doe eyes held concern.

He shrugged. "But since Joy left me, I've been working through that issue as well. I was angry my birth mother didn't want me. I was mad Mom and Dad didn't tell me I was adopted. A big part of me felt deceived and abandoned—the same feelings I fought through when Joy up and left."

"That must have been such a shock to learn." She touched his arm.

"I don't think they ever told me because they never thought about it. My mother's sister is my biological mother. I guess since I came to them as an infant, in their mind, I was theirs. Period. But at times… I guess I don't feel like a real McCaw."

"Oh, Ethan. Cora and Wade don't treat you any different from Autumn or your brothers. You have three, right?"

"Yes. Austin, Carter and Walker." He shook off the topic, unsure why he'd even brought it up. He gazed at the tiny two-story. "So, if the house is for the bride and groom to get ready for their big day, where are you going to live?"

"Eventually, I'd like to build a small home beyond the grove of trees over there." She pointed to a space not far away, which would allow her privacy from the venue but let her be close enough that she could be here in a moment's time.

Her chipped nails, now with only sections of the watermelon pink, were much different than the perfect manicure from the other day. Would she go into town and get a manicure at the salon every week or two? The city life seemed deeply ingrained in her.

"But for now, I'll hole up on the second floor. I can use the kitchen when there aren't events." A peaceful smile lifted her plump lips. "Otherwise, a coffee maker, microwave and dorm-size fridge in the front bedroom will suffice."

"Sorry I treated you like an annoyance when we were kids." He might have been a bit harsh to her in their childhood.

She laughed. "So you *do* remember me."

He sure did. Back then, she'd been an annoying friend of his sister's, but she'd grown up. Though from her demeanor, she seemed as broken as he. Bits and pieces of her childhood floated around in his mind, but he didn't have the complete story.

"You always wanted to help at the camp, and I never let you. Sorry about that." He moved the wand to a new section of siding.

Ace sidled up to her, and she leaned over to massage his head.

"I forgive you." She glanced at her phone. "As soon as we're done, I need to work on a website. An old coworker of mine is about to start his own business and isn't great with computers. So I offered to help him."

"I didn't realize you had so much free time."

She shot him a pointed look. "He's paying me. I can use every spare dollar for this renovation. Especially after this morning's plumbing incident."

He continued methodically spraying the side of the house. He recognized a restless person when he met one. Or at least now he did. His ex-wife always had one foot out the door, just like Laney seemed to. During Joy's pregnancy, she couldn't wait for the twins to arrive. He'd assumed she was excited about meeting them. Instead, after she gave birth, she'd exercised constantly, trying to get her body back in shape. No, Laney wasn't being selfish with her restless behavior, but like Joy, he was pretty sure Laney would end up back in the city.

Ace dropped the tennis ball at her feet, then backed up. She picked up the ball and threw it. The dog raced after it and Laney grinned at his antics.

His stomach clenched at her fun-loving nature.

How had he allowed himself to agree to spend so much time with this enchanting woman?

Ever since Joy abandoned him, he had absolutely no intention of another relationship, especially with a city gal. Yet against his better judgment he was looking forward to getting to know Laney better.

And that awareness terrified him.

Chapter Five

Monday morning, tires crunched over gravel on the driveway.

Laney yawned at the outrageous hour and stepped onto the dark porch. After years of working in event planning, she'd turned into a bona fide night owl. True to his word, Ethan had arrived closer to six thirty, likely cutting it close getting to the ranch by dawn. Though that was sweet of him, now she was second-guessing babysitting the girls. Getting up this early every day would grow old quick, especially with how late she was up last night peeling wallpaper from the powder room walls.

However, Ethan had proved his worth on Saturday. He definitely knew about construction and would be a bigger help than she'd originally anticipated. So maybe *she* was getting the better end of the bargain? She plastered on a smile and met him on the porch.

Ace scrambled through the door behind her as Ethan climbed the steps, one girl asleep in his arms.

She opened the door for him and rushed into the living room to clear space on the loaner couch. Thankfully Cora had insisted she use their garage apartment sofa while Laney's soggy couch sat in the garage to dry out. "I had forgotten the girls would still be sleeping. I am so sorry about this."

Gently, he laid Tori down. She knew who it was because the girl wore short-sleeve purple pajamas.

"No worries. I move them in and out of their car seats often when they are sleeping. It's part of being a single parent, I guess, so it isn't an inconvenience." He quickly returned with a pink-clad Zoe.

He handled them like fine china and it hit Laney how difficult it must be as a cattle rancher and a single father. Two tasks that required much time and effort. Her admiration of him grew.

"Thank you again for agreeing to watch my munchkins." He smiled, then said, "I have a few instructions for you."

He had moved her computer and cables off to the side of the kitchen table and dropped two frayed bags and a thick notebook in their place. He rubbed his chin, drawing her attention to the growing stubble. Very attractive.

"In here are extra clothes and some pull-ups. We are working on potty training but haven't gotten there just yet." He shrugged and pointed at the hunter green reusable grocery tote. "Snacks. I'll be back by eleven. Promise."

Then he opened the notebook and pointed out emergency contacts and foods they liked and disliked. One page even listed activity suggestions broken out in fifteen-minute increments.

The moisture in her mouth dried as the enormity of her morning task sank in. She wasn't prepared to be left alone with these girls. What would she do if something horrible happened?

She had been nervous about watching them before, but the sight of this gigantic book of notes overwhelmed her. Why had she accepted this job? She drew a shaky hand over her suddenly sweaty forehead.

"Questions?"

She shook her head, dumbfounded at the situation she found herself in.

"I'll leave my truck here with the car seats

in case you need to go anywhere or if there is an emergency." He chuckled. "An ambulance takes a while to arrive out here, so just drive into town if anything happens." He raised his brows. "Can I borrow your car to get back to the ranch?"

An ambulance? She gulped and grabbed her car fob from the key hook. What had she gotten herself into?

After he drove away, she peeked at the sleeping girls. They looked so harmless in their pj's, their blond hair disheveled. On her way to coffee, she passed her aunt's marked-up Bible. She'd get to her daily reading later. These past few days, being in Serenity and reading God's Word, had given her an extra measure of peace.

In the kitchen, she rooted around and found the bag of grounds and filled the water reservoir. As the coffee brewed, she inhaled the aroma. Not as good as her French press back in the city, but it was better than nothing.

As dawn broke, she wrapped her hands around a steaming mug and took her first sip, reveling in the taste and warmth. She glanced at the couch. The sleeping girls were gone.

Her eyes widened. *Where'd they go?*

Suddenly she heard giggling from down the hall. She released the worried breath she hadn't realized she'd been holding and scurried to them.

The twins were washing their hands. Innocent and sweet. They both hugged Laney and thanked her for letting them come over. *See, today will be fine.*

She was thankful the plumber had come out yesterday afternoon and fixed the broken pipe, otherwise she would have had to watch the girls at Ethan's. Unfortunately, the plumber had discovered that the galvanized pipes were corroded and needed to be replaced throughout the house. The first cost overage for her construction project that hadn't even officially started.

Before she knew it, the girls began racing around the kitchen, then the living and dining rooms. What if one of them fell on the buckling hardwood floors, got hurt and she had to drive them to the clinic? She didn't know how to buckle a toddler into a car seat.

Worry clawed at her chest. She should have asked Ethan for a crash course on safety. Better yet, she should have observed him unbuckling them this morning. Why hadn't she thought of that a half hour ago?

The giggles that at first sounded cute had become loud screeches and screams as their feet pounded over the hardwood floors.

Laney rushed to the kitchen table and Ethan's bags of goodies. Soft breakfast bars. Juice boxes.

"Girls, it's time for breakfast." She had to get them seated and calmed down. She wiped her sweaty palms on her pants. What had made her think watching them here was a good idea? This place wasn't childproofed, and there were no toys.

Tori darted past. "I only like the red ones." She dashed away.

Laney dug in the bag—sure enough, there were bars with red wrappers. She dropped the blue ones in the bag and grabbed two reds.

The next time Tori raced by, she snatched one. "Thanks," she called over her shoulder.

"I want a blue one." Zoe clung to Laney's thigh.

Before she knew it, both girls were at her side, each chewing a breakfast bar. She shoved straws into the juice pouches. "Why don't you share a chair? And drink this."

They climbed onto the chair, both panting from the exertion.

Laney rummaged through the bag for the banana she'd seen, split it in half and gave each girl a piece. After she wiped her hands, she sank against the counter and sipped her now-lukewarm coffee. She was used to multitasking at her day job. Massaging hurt feelings. Making difficult decisions.

Handling a pair of three-year-olds should be a piece of cake. Except, why did she feel as unqualified today as she had ten years ago on her first day as an event planner assistant?

"You're it." Zoe poked Tori and then ran off. Tori followed. And it started again.

Laney's stomach turned at their constant motion and her inability to multitask while watching them. If they kept this up, she wouldn't be able to peel wallpaper, let alone work on the website design like she had hoped.

Ace's damp nose nudged her, and a brilliant idea formed. "Girls, let's go outside." She walked to the door, hoping they'd follow. When she spotted a can of spray paint on top of the fridge, she grabbed it.

Once outside, the girls ran free in what looked like a safer environment. Except she didn't want them running too far away or into the chaotic barn because they could hurt themselves. She also remembered the copperhead that bit Ace, so she shook the can and sprayed orange Xs in four corners of the sheared grass, creating a makeshift fence to try to keep them safe.

"Stay inside the orange, girls." She'd handled brides with strong opinions. She could handle a couple of toddlers, couldn't she?

Ace raced around with them for a couple of minutes, then retreated to the deck and sprawled in the shade.

"I'm hot." Zoe bolted up the steps and into the house, red-faced and sweaty.

"Me, too." Tori trailed close behind.

A lump lodged in Laney's throat at her incompetence to manage them. She rushed to follow. Well, that worked for five minutes. What was she supposed to do for the next four hours?

To keep them contained, she closed and then locked the stairwell leading to the bedrooms, then barricaded the dining room opening. That left the kitchen and living space for the girls to run around in, much more manageable. Laney stood in a corner where she could assure their safety as they continued chasing each other.

Their energy appeared never-ending, but finally, they both landed on the couch, panting and giggling. Laney offered them juice boxes, which they readily drank.

While seated and somewhat calm, she handed them each a magnet playset she'd found on top of the fridge that she had played with when she was little. Seemed her aunt had saved several of Laney's old toys, and she was grateful for that.

They tossed their drinks aside, placed the tin playset on their laps and lifted the hinged lids. Apparently, Aunt Alice had shared these with them in the past, because they knew the inside of the imprinted play scene on the box lid served as the stage. They began sticking magnetic dolls and accessories on the stage as they explored their imaginations.

Laney breathed a sigh of relief. Now, this she could handle.

Even though she craved a nap, she forced herself to multitask like she had planned. She settled on her uncle's recliner that had weathered the burst pipe and kept the girls in view while she worked on finishing her new client's website.

As she experimented with different fonts to make the page look more professional, she became engrossed with the site. When she glanced at the couch, the girls had vanished, the contents of their tin playsets strewn on the floor. Again. Laney jumped up and rushed to the kitchen.

The twins sat in a pile of flour and sugar they

had emptied onto the kitchen floor. The ripped paper containers lay strewn behind them.

Her gut jolted at the sight. *No.* "Stop right there."

Their eyes held surprise at her stern warning.

Zoe gripped a container of sprinkles and, as though Laney hadn't spoken, dumped them into the pile. Then she used a wooden spoon to stir.

"I sowwy," Tori apologized as she poured a measuring cup of water onto the concoction. Some of the liquid seeped into the mound, the rest dribbling off. "We couldn't find a bowl."

How come Laney couldn't keep the girls under control? Her head pounded as she tugged them to the bathroom to wash their hands and dust off the sugar and flour from their clothing.

This was way harder than she'd ever expected. Now that she knew the twins were lightning quick, she needed to keep her eye on them at all times.

"I wanted to make a mastewpiece," Zoe explained, as they passed the mound on the kitchen floor.

Laney gritted her teeth at the mess. Well, she'd known this place wasn't childproofed when she offered to nanny, but she hadn't realized how much of a problem that would be. She settled them at the table and gave them dry-erase boards she had found in Ethan's magical bag.

Once the twins were absorbed with writing on the boards, Laney did her best to clean the kitchen mess, but the goo stuck between the warped floorboards like cement. They hadn't played with one thing for more than ten minutes, but these dry-erase boards kept them occupied. Maybe all those online seminars she had taken on redirecting people were finally paying off.

Her phone beeped. It was Autumn. Because of budget, how about we make the surprise party a potluck?

Laney rolled her eyes and settled in a kitchen chair next to the girls. This is a special anniversary party for your parents. I'll work something out for the food.

Maybe we could use the camp building? Autumn texted.

No. Somewhere special. How about the town square? A trio can play country music. If we start around seven, then at dusk those romantic overhead lights will turn on. Your mom will love it. Laney smiled at the idea.

You are amazing, yes and yes. I'll coordinate with the town. My brother Walker knows a trio. I'll ask him to book them. Autumn ended the exchange with a happy hugging emoji.

Laney began to hum a song she'd heard last night while removing wallpaper. This little party was coming together nicely. It felt good to be in charge of the event. Better than she thought it would. She tucked her phone away.

"I'm the housekeeper. You're the guest," Tori stated.

"But I want to dust." Zoe stomped her foot.

Laney jumped up. Her chest tightened at the new mess. "Give me the hair spray." The tension in her voice banged around the kitchen, landing beneath her rib cage.

How had she forgotten about the girls again? She reached out and snatched the can from Tori.

The twins froze, as though they knew they had pushed too far this time.

The girls had used her hair spray to "dust," and now the house was a sticky dust ball.

Regret over accepting this bartering deal with Ethan knifed at her. Along with the peeling and buckling hardwood floors, the place was officially a disaster zone.

She spotted scribbling on the walls and her shoulders crumpled. She hadn't planned to paint the sunny yellow kitchen, but now she'd have to.

As she scrutinized the space that used to be picked up and presentable, tears welled up in her eyes. Why had she thought she could take care of toddlers all by herself? This morning had turned into a nightmare.

She collapsed to the ground. The awareness that she was a failure started a pounding behind her eyes. She couldn't do this—she couldn't be a nanny. And if she couldn't watch the girls for Ethan, then he wouldn't help her with the renovation.

And she *needed* him. If she didn't complete her to-do list, then she'd have to borrow even more money for this renovation.

The tears flowed. She heard hiccuping. It must have been her, but she was past caring.

Tori and Zoe ran over to her. They patted her on her back and arm, told her everything would be okay.

Their compassion only made her cry harder.

Apparently, there was no such thing as control when watching a pair of toddlers.

Exhausted from a long morning working on the ranch, Ethan arrived at Laney's house, expecting to hear laughter or giggling. Instead, his twins were wailing.

Concern shot through his chest. He hurried through the screen door and into the messy living room. In the corner, Laney sat against the wood paneling, hugging her knees, a twin clinging to each arm. He rushed over and crouched in front of them.

Laney was bawling. Both girls had tearstained cheeks.

"What happened? Is someone hurt?" Worry tore at him as he took in the scene.

"Th-they emptied all the sugar," she stuttered and stammered, "and the f-flour on the floor. Then added sprinkles and water." She sucked in a couple of breaths and then continued. "It was the worst gooey mess to clean up. They even wrote on the walls." Her gaze met his. "Then they used hair spray to dust everything."

He surveyed the space. Yes, there was more of a mess than earlier in the day. He sank to the floor, and his girls rushed over to him, clinging to his neck. When they settled down fairly quickly, relief replaced the tension in his body.

Then he reached out and touched Laney.

"I'm a failure," she mumbled.

"No. You. Are. Not." He should have stopped by to check on them midmorning. If he had, maybe things wouldn't have escalated. "I should have warned you. My girls like to push the envelope with new people."

Instead of taking the safe route and moving across the room, he thumbed away a tear streaming down her face and gazed into her ocean-blue eyes. The moment hung in the air. Maybe he should have kept his hands to himself. But she was so upset. So vulnerable. How had he ended up with such an attractive nanny?

"A pair of toddlers are a challenge, but the good times are worth it." Her watery gaze didn't look convinced.

She swiped at her eyes, her perfect pink manicure gone. Her nails were now bare, several broken, most likely from removing the stubborn bathroom wallpaper. Though, just because the manicure was gone didn't mean her city-gal tendencies had disappeared.

He recalled the quick hug she'd given him during Pops in the Park. How it made him feel accepted. And stirred up feelings he wished would go away.

After the disastrous end to his marriage, he'd thought he might never date again. He'd learned at an early age that some people who were supposed to love him didn't stay. His birth mother and his ex-wife had left him. He wasn't about to walk that road again. He shifted back a little to make space between them.

"I know it's hard, but you can do this," he whispered. She seemed to hang on to each word. And somehow they calmed her. "How about if we take the girls back to my house for lunch and I can feed you, too?" The girls had loosened their grip, their heads now snuggled against his chest.

She glanced at him, her sad eyes filled with tears. "Okay."

Once back at his house, he made quick sandwiches for lunch. Laney seemed a bit zoned out and ate little. After he put the twins down for their nap, he returned to the kitchen.

Laney was pacing and wringing her hands. "I'm so sorry."

"It is not your fault. They are little terrors sometimes. This morning was one of those times." He pulled a face. "I should have warned you. But if I had, I don't think you would have accepted the deal."

Her blue-green eyes gazed up at him.

He turned to rinse the lunch dishes in the sink. "I should be the one apologizing, not you. If they damaged anything that needs to be replaced, I'm good for it."

She sighed. "You are so kind. But it's clear I'm not responsible enough to care for your girls. I'm sure you understand."

Wait. What? He turned the faucet off and swiveled to study her. "You're not quitting, are you?" His voice rose with disbelief.

"It's the best thing for everyone." Her face scrunched up like she was going to cry again. "I'll just have to hire a handyman."

His stomach clenched as he crossed the room. "No, you don't understand. They were just testing you. It'll get easier from now on." He was proud of his independent and determined girls. Except for today. Their behavior might have cost him his only childcare option.

"I can't take care of the girls. It's too hard." She stepped back. "I didn't have a good example." A haunting look passed through her.

He remembered Autumn telling him that she and Laney had many deep conversations. His sister had even shared with Ethan about Laney's alcoholic mother, who relied on every man she ever met.

"No, Laney, that's where you're wrong. Your mother doesn't define you. You had Arthur and Alice. And my mom and dad. You can draw from those positive experiences."

Her gaze softened. Perhaps trying to figure out if she should take that and run with it or assume that since her mother was a failure, she would be as well.

"From my viewpoint, you're doing great." Yes, he didn't want to lose her as a nanny, but he also thought Laney had promise. The girls really liked her, and she seemed to like them.

"Today was horrible."

"So it can't get any worse, right?" Yesterday at church, Laney had looked beautiful. But today, with messy hair, cheeks ruddy from crying and totally out of her element, her beauty was more evident. She wore hard work well. Really well.

She cocked her head. "Maybe?"

He chuckled. "They've broken you in. It'll get easier from here on out. I promise."

Hope lined her features as she gazed up at him. "You think so?"

"Absolutely. And I'll be at your place at three to demo that wall."

"Well, then, tomorrow I'll just watch them here. Your house has all their toys, and it's childproofed."

The trust on her face evoked a childhood memory of when he'd gone fishing, and the occasions when she and Autumn had joined him. And the many times he coached her on her horseback-riding skills. She was a natural and hadn't required much help.

He took a step back, because right now, he needed to be careful and not get too attached.

A scream pierced the quiet. Tori.

Panic took hold as he rushed into the girls' bedroom. Tori lay in a crumpled heap at the base of their tall bookcase. Had she climbed to the top and fallen off?

When she spotted him, the earsplitting wail intensified. She stood, holding her left elbow as Zoe lay sound asleep in her toddler bed. His heart hammered. Was Tori hurt?

But if she could stand, and her arm wasn't in an awkward position, most likely nothing was broken, right?

Maybe she was just scared. He scooped her up and took her into the hallway, sliding the door closed behind him.

Her cries turned to whimpers. "I fell."

"Think it's broken?" Laney stood a few feet away, concern etched on her face.

One look at Laney and Tori's cries intensified. Rattled, he felt along his daughter's arm, but she pulled away and grimaced when he got near her elbow. "I think she needs to see a doctor. Or maybe go to the urgent care."

"Go," Laney stated. "I'll stay here with Zoe until you get back."

How his girls had gotten this old without breaking anything was beyond him, but today might be the day for their first cast. "Okay.

You've got my cell number. And my mom is at the big house."

Worry replaced panic as he grabbed his wallet and keys, rushing out the door with Tori on his hip. Then he loaded her into her car seat and pointed his truck toward the urgent care. No way could he call the doctor with a howling child in the car.

As he traversed the roads, his pulse raced in his throat. Inconsolable, Tori wailed. He prayed that her arm was easily mendable and would return to normal soon.

Same for his life. His feelings for Laney alarmed him and he wanted his regular uncomplicated world back.

Chapter Six

Saturday afternoon, Ethan slid into an angled parking spot across from What's the Scoop. He hopped down from the truck, opened the passenger door, then leaned into the back to free the girls from their car seats. "Remember, we need to make a line."

"Yes, Daddy." Obedience wasn't their strong suit, but somehow they seemed to understand safety around cars, cows and horses. He was still working on pools, roosters and heights.

The sun shone bright as he helped them step onto the running board. Once they jumped to the ground, Zoe grasped Tori's hand, and he held Zoe's. This was their usual "line" when out in public and near traffic. Thankfully, it worked with Tori's sprained arm, which was in a bright purple sling until Monday.

This week had gone better than expected. Sure, Laney's first day babysitting had been a disaster. But each day it had gotten better for the girls and easier for Laney. She was a fun nanny who made obedience a game for the twins, and he enjoyed helping her with the renovations. And after reinstating his daily quiet time with God this past week, he was thankful for the extra peace and grace as he went about each day.

They stepped onto the sidewalk. "I am so proud of both of you."

"We big girls." Tori skipped forward.

"Ice cweam for lunch," Zoe stated.

His girls were growing up, whether he liked it or not.

"Lane!" Tori broke free and scampered toward Laney, who strode toward them on the sidewalk. Zoe followed.

Laney grinned as she crouched low and hugged them, being cautious of Tori's sling. "What's the occasion?" She lifted a hand to shield her eyes from the sun. Her smile was wide and intriguing.

It warmed him to see how excited the twins were to see Laney. And even though he'd read trepidation in her eyes after that first day of nannying, she'd persevered, and the week had gone very well. Now she appeared comfortable playing with them, and they were smitten with her.

"Ice cream," they triumphantly cheered.

She looked at him and cocked her head. "Isn't it a little early?"

"We're celebrating." He winked. "Someone used the potty."

She clapped and focused on the girls. "Who?" Her gaze darted between them.

"Both of us."

She threw her head back and laughed. "Of course. I should have guessed. Good for both of you." She looked at him. "Job well done."

Oh, she did not know what hoops he'd jumped through to make that happen an hour ago.

What stuck in his mind was her captivating laugh. And how the sound affected him.

"Join us. When's the last time you had ice cream for lunch?"

Her eyes lit up. "I can't think of when. Maybe never?" She smiled. "I'd love to."

The girls hopped up and down, and then each took one of Laney's hands.

After Joy had left him, even speaking to a single woman had made him nervous. On Sundays, they'd flock to him and the girls after church. He'd tried to be cordial, because he didn't want to send the wrong signal to anyone. But chatting with Laney differed completely from interacting with any other woman.

He opened What's the Scoop's door. "Ladies first."

The twins dropped Laney's hands and rushed to the glass cooler, still not tall enough to see the flavors.

"Morning, Otto," he greeted the proprietor, then lifted Zoe. Laney picked up Tori, being careful with her hurt arm. "Thanks."

As the girls oohed and aahed over their selections, Laney frowned. "Zoe, why do you have purple on?"

His mouth fell open at her observation. Zoe always wore pink. Tori was his purple gal.

He chuckled. "They insisted on swapping this morning. I'm surprised you could tell them apart."

She smiled. "I could tell these girls apart if they both had blue on."

He put Zoe back on the ground as Laney released a now-squirming Tori.

"We girls. We not wear blue." Zoe scowled at Laney. Blue, red and yellow were colors they refused to wear. Something in Laney's expression must have softened Zoe's reaction, because his little girls hugged their new nanny like she'd been a part of their lives forever.

His heart squeezed. In one short week, the twins had fallen for Laney.

"Laney Taylor, is that you?" Otto asked.

Her cheeks creased. "Yes, it is. How have you been, Otto?"

A brief exchange was not what Otto had in mind. No, he came out from behind the counter to wrap Laney in a bear hug and tell her how much he'd missed her, then spent a few minutes catching up with her.

"Gween, please," Zoe stated.

"Purple," Tori announced.

Otto scooped their ice cream into sugar cones coated with chocolate and sprinkles. Ethan ordered butter pecan.

"I have a special treat for you," Otto told Laney. "Just give me a minute." He moved to the deep freezer.

They all settled in a booth, preferring the air-conditioning to the humidity outside. The girls wanted to sit next to each other in the booth, so Laney settled right beside him. Their legs almost touched. If he moved about an inch to his left, they would. Except he stayed right where he was. Safe.

"So, what are you doing in town?" She appeared more relaxed than when she'd first arrived in Serenity.

"I've hit some local shops, like Eatalian Pizza and Morning Grind, and negotiated a deep discount for the anniversary party food."

"Why don't we do a potluck?"

"No." Her wavy hair bounced as she shook her head. "We want the food and location to be special, not dishes Cora and Wade are familiar with from regular church events."

"Is this within budget?" His brow furrowed. This event-planning thing was not in his wheelhouse.

"Autumn gave me the budget. I negotiated a deal for food at cost and, in exchange, cards along the buffet will describe what it is and display their business name." She shrugged. "It's a win-win for everyone. They get some advertising, and we get yummy food at a deep discount."

"I'm impressed, Laney. You're very creative. I bet your wedding venue will be a big hit."

A flush crept up her cheeks. "Oh, I forgot to tell you. We decided to have the anniversary party in the town square. Autumn finally got approval."

He nodded his support. "This party will be

much more special with you at the helm, rather than me or Autumn or one of my brothers."

Out of the corner of his eye, he saw Zoe's pistachio scoop fall off her cone, hit the edge of the table and land on the bench seat next to her. Zoe's cry rumbled low like a slow-moving train at first, and then hit fever pitch as she banged her heels against the seat in frustration.

He attempted to gather her into a hug, but she pushed him away.

All the while, Laney scooped the ice cream into a cup and mopped the sticky wetness away from Zoe with a wad of napkins.

He tried to calm Zoe down, but nothing he did worked.

After tossing everything into the trash can, Laney slid back onto the bench seat, and Zoe flung herself into Laney's chest. Laney engulfed her in a hug and rubbed her back, whispering words of encouragement.

In shock, Ethan leaned back. For three years, he'd been Zoe's only source of comfort. Sure, his parents stepped in sometimes, but Laney?

His ribs grew tight. He wasn't jealous of Laney, was he?

No. He yearned for his girls to rely on many adults for wisdom, encouragement and comfort, not just him. So why was he disappointed he wasn't Zoe's first choice today?

Zoe's sobs slowed to a whimper. Soon enough, Laney walked both the girls over to the play area, then slid back into the seat.

"Thanks for that." He tilted his head at Zoe. "Someday you'll make a wonderful mother."

"I don't know." She wrinkled her nose. "That's not really my plan. Think you'll ever remarry?"

Her question threw him for a moment. "No. I mean, Joy leaving was hard on me. I couldn't imagine going through love and a possible breakup with the girls in tow. Especially now that they are older and more aware of what is happening."

She gazed up at him and he got lost in her wide blue-green pools.

"I'm sorry she left."

He stilled. Were they becoming friends? Did he even want a woman as a friend? Except, he knew having a strong female influence for his daughters would be good. And Laney planned to stick around Serenity, so even after the nannying gig, she'd be there for his girls. Just like the rest of the community, right?

A strange energy hummed in the air around them as Laney collected the stray napkins and threw them in the trash. When she sat back down, her presence tempted him to lean closer to her.

"Thanks for helping demo the wall yesterday. That was fun."

He'd watched YouTube videos for hours after the twins were in bed to prepare before showing up the other afternoon. "No problem. Is Steve going to be able to relocate the HVAC?"

"I think so. For a price." She crumpled a napkin in her hand, worried it, strangled it.

He covered her hand with his. "Don't worry. I'm confident we can accomplish everything on that to-do list stuck to your fridge."

Her gaze met his. "I'm afraid I may have overcommitted."

"We can do it." A sudden plan developed. A community workday. For Laney. He'd start making calls tonight.

She pulled her hand away. "How's camp going?"

"Great—thanks for asking. My mother's in her glory. Exhausted every evening." He leaned back. "Attendance is at capacity, but all the committed volunteers are showing up like they promised."

Otto waddled over with a single scoop on a cone. "Laney, try this." He handed her the cone.

"Is this coffee caramel fudge?" She grinned.

"Sure is. As soon as I saw you at Pops in the Park, I thought about this flavor and made it up the next day." His eyes sparkled. "Just grabbed it from the freezer. Now there's a whole bucket for when you come back next. Enjoy." Otto returned to the counter.

The corners of Laney's mouth tipped up. "He is so sweet." She took a bite. "Mmm, this is good."

A bit of caramel stuck to Laney's chin. Without thinking, Ethan swiped it away with his thumb. Her eyes widened at his touch.

He froze as his senses leaped to life.

He never should have touched her. Should have ignored the caramel sticking to her chin.

His heart drummed against his rib cage at their closeness.

Being near Laney opened up emotions he'd thought he'd never have again. Feelings he'd never expected to resurface.

He was attracted to Laney, but he didn't want to be. He needed to get back to cattle ranching, caring for his twins and enjoying family dinners at the big house.

Uncomplicated. Simple. Unemotional.

Somehow, he had to chase away the building attraction. He just wasn't sure how.

Or if it might be too late.

* * *

Laney's heartbeat raced as Ethan's intense gaze locked on hers. The door chimed, breaking the moment. Someone must have entered the shop.

Her pulse slowly returned to normal. What had just happened? Was he developing feelings for her? Was she?

No. She tossed the unwelcome notion aside.

A new customer chatted with Otto. The girls' voices lifted as they played in the children's corner.

Ethan broke the silence. "Your ice cream is dripping."

She jerked her head back and shifted her cone away. A quick glance down revealed a series of coffee caramel drips on the front of her white dress. She groaned.

What a fool to be taken in by a man's charms. She shook her head, tossed out the cone and grabbed a handful of napkins.

"Here's some club soda." A worried Otto hustled over and handed her a foam cup and a clean towel.

She dipped the towel in the bubbly liquid and rubbed, but instead of cleaning it off, she created a circular mess on the center of her pretty new dress. How embarrassing. Head down, she returned to the booth.

"Do you really want a nanny who spills ice cream?" she asked, grinning. Though all she wanted was to go home. Change. Forget this embarrassing moment had ever happened.

He chuckled. "No, Laney, you're doing great. The kids love you. I…" He seemed at a loss for words. "I'm happy with you. I mean, with how you are with the kids." Heat rose in his cheeks as he looked at the girls.

He was as uncomfortable as she was.

After what Ethan had been through with his ex-wife, of course he wasn't looking for another relationship. Him wiping the ice cream off her chin meant nothing. Anyone would have done that, right?

Except she couldn't forget the butterflies in her belly that had taken flight when he touched her.

Right now, though, she needed to leave. Get home and try to rescue this dress before someone other than Ethan saw her and the situation became more embarrassing.

The girls rushed to the table. Their curly blond hair hung free today. "Can we go to 'Mation Station, please?" Their brilliant blue eyes sparkled with excitement.

The skin around Ethan's eyes crinkled.

"Imagination Station. As long as you know we aren't buying anything today."

Excellent—she had a way out without offending the twins. How fast could she get to her car?

When they got to the sidewalk, Laney smiled. "Well, thanks for the ice cream. I'll probably see you all at church in the morning." She held her purse in front of the stain, though the leather barely covered the huge spot.

Tori and Zoe each grabbed on to one of her elbows. "No, you've gotta see the dollhouse at the store. Daddy, pwease?"

He shrugged. "Sure." Then he tossed Laney a conspiratorial look.

Her heart sank. She didn't want to walk around town like this. But how could she say no to the girls? "Okay. But just for a few minutes." Maybe her purse hid the coffee-colored smudge?

Satisfied, the girls released her elbows and rushed ahead, the sound of their giggles lifting in the air.

"Thank you for planning my parents' anniversary party." He waved to a Serenity resident. "I've been thinking about how you've thrown yourself into this event. You love your job, like

I do. So I think you know how I feel about that land," he said firmly.

He was right. Not only did she enjoy planning events, but this surprise party for Cora and Wade had differed completely from her usual events. She'd been having sleep-filled nights, no stress. This party almost felt like a different type of job than her old position.

Her mind shifted to the fields he leased closest to her house and venue. The areas she'd been considering for a ceremony location. "Do you water the pastures you lease?" she asked. Out of all the areas on her property, those two fields were so lush and green, they'd make the prettiest backdrop for a wedding ceremony.

"Yes. We use a center pivot to irrigate, since we don't get regular rain around here." His eyes glowed with the ranch talk.

"Is that the big metal contraptions on wheels that I used to see watering the cotton fields when I was a kid?"

Ethan graced her with a wide smile. "Yup. You sure remember the summer months you spent here." He shifted his Stetson on his head. "Watering those pastures takes manpower." His tone had turned hard. "Which is why it'd be a blow to lose any of the land we've worked so hard on." Worry swam in his eyes.

Her gut wrenched at the thought of possibly being the one to rip that away from him and his family. He might want to discuss the lease, but she wasn't about to make any promises right now. She pinched her lips together as they followed the girls in silence.

As the construction project began, she had come to the conclusion that she'd need the monthly payments from the contract renewal. So, unfortunately, she didn't have a choice but to find a way to work with the McCaws. Especially because so many things were popping up with the renovation that the cost kept rising.

She shoved those unpleasant thoughts into the back of her brain as laughter from the girls up ahead filtered back.

Sadly, every nugget of information she learned about how the McCaws used Arthur's land put a nail in the coffin of taking it away from them. There had to be a way to continue the lease and for her to still have a professional wedding venue on the same land. But the incident with the escaped cow bothered her. And, unfortunately, it hadn't been an isolated event.

The problem was, Cora and Wade had done too much for her over the years. And Ethan—well, he'd gone above and beyond. Repeatedly.

They passed through the Imagination Station door. An hour ago, she'd sensed she was interfering with family time. Now she felt like a part of them. But instead of liking the image, it disturbed her.

Once in the toy store, the girls pulled her toward a wooden dollhouse perched on a display table that was children's height. As they told her all about the rooms and the dolls that lived there, their voices rose and they lifted onto their toes.

Laney shared in their excitement. In the middle of moving the furniture around, Laney realized she deeply cared about Zoe and Tori. When these six weeks ended, she'd miss them. A lot.

"How was babysitting this past week? I see you're still alive."

She peered up at Ethan. "Rough but rewarding." Tori and Zoe were a joy to be with, unless they were getting into trouble. And trouble could be their middle name.

"I get that."

Her structured workaholic days from San Antonio had turned upside down. "At first, I was concerned about getting up so early to watch the girls. I worried I'd be too exhausted in the evenings to work on the house. Except, I've found the twins almost seem to invigorate me."

"Same here." His eyes twinkled.

"Can I help you with anything?" a teenage employee, who wore an apron with the toy store's emblem wrapped around her waist, asked.

Laney moved her purse to cover the ice cream stain—or at least tried to. "Oh, no, we're just playing. Is that okay?"

The friendly employee smiled. "Sure thing." She straightened the sale sign sitting on the roof. "I love when parents play with their children. It's cute."

Laney froze as the girl walked away. She wanted to correct the teen, but she didn't want to say anything to offend the girls, so she kept quiet.

A family. The employee thought they were a family. Laney gulped.

When Ethan glanced her way, her pulse stuttered. Yup, she was starting to like him. But she pushed those feelings away. They'd never amount to anything worthwhile.

She looked away from his chiseled face. Attraction led to feelings. And feelings led to nothing good. If she'd only learned one thing from her mother, that was it.

But there was something about Ethan that intrigued her in ways that panicked her.

Even though she'd fallen for the twins, she didn't want the same to happen with Ethan. Her judgment of character was a little off. Well, a lot.

If she didn't stay focused on providing for herself, she'd get derailed and lose everything. And now, as she started her own business, that was more important than ever.

Somehow, she needed to create some distance between herself and Ethan. But how?

Zoe tugged on her hand, pulling her back into their play world.

Maybe she shouldn't have returned to Serenity—then she never would have reconnected with Ethan.

Because whatever was happening between them warned her that she could never go back.

Never return to the city life.

Never return to the emotionless life she had led before.

And that frightened her.

Chapter Seven

In Ethan's backyard, Laney relaxed in one of his plastic garden chairs, exhausted from her Thursday morning with the girls. Almost two weeks down, four more to go. She kicked off her flip-flops and spread her toes over the warm grass while the twins played with chalk on the concrete patio. The rain last night had created a clean slate for today.

Zoe stuck her tongue out of the corner of her mouth, proving she was concentrating hard, as she drew a figure with orange chalk. Maybe a horse? Or a dog? Maybe the house?

"Good job, Zoe." At barely three years old, just keeping chalk to concrete was a success.

The girl gave her a shy smile.

"What about mine?" Tori backed away from her purple-squiggly masterpiece.

Laney squatted and enveloped Tori in a side hug, thankful the sling was gone and her elbow no longer hurt. "Yours is great, too." Looking at the two masterpieces, set off from the earlier scribbling, gave her an idea.

"Do you know what the big *T* and *Z* on the wall in your bedroom stand for?"

"*T* is for Tori and *Z* is for Zoe," they harmonized.

Laney grinned. "You're right. Look." On the patio, she wrote a block *T* under Tori's drawing and a *Z* under Zoe's for each of their names. "See how simple that is? Try to write the letter beside where I did."

While they worked on their letters, Laney took in Ethan's small house, surrounded front and back with a white picket fence. It was her dream home on the outside, but as it turned out, she adored the inside as well. There was enough space, but not too much. It was decorated in a rustic and casual manner, just like Ethan. And had plenty of outdoor space to play.

When the girls had completed their letters, Laney clapped. "Good job." She used a damp finger to erase her letters. "Now you've signed your artwork."

They appeared pleased with themselves.

A smile touched Laney's lips when she recalled her first day as a nanny. What a disaster. That first day, Ethan had wrapped her in his arms and comforted her, the scent of horses and hay clinging to him. His strong arms had soothed her, and his sweet words had encouraged and lifted her up.

Had they only reconnected five days before that? Sometimes, when her friendship with Ethan came to mind, she had a hard time believing they'd only been close for a few weeks. Something about being with him was so comfortable it put Laney at ease.

She used a damp paper towel to erase the errant scribblings on the patio, leaving just the two masterpieces and their block letters to show Ethan. After they selected new colors, the girls started a fresh drawing. Today Laney had found time to put together a healthy lunch for everyone, including turkey roll-ups, fresh fruit and the banana bread Cora had dropped off on her way to camp earlier. Now they were waiting for Ethan to arrive home to eat.

Zoe discarded her chalk and headed to her tricycle. In mere moments, Tori followed suit.

"Can we visit the chickens, Lane?" Tori climbed off her tricycle.

"Please?" Zoe wheeled over and looked up at her with such a sweet, angelic face.

Ethan had told her several times they weren't to go into the chicken coop alone, because the rooster was aggressive around young children. There was no way she would take them to see the chickens. "How about after lunch, when your daddy is home?"

They shrugged and went over to their giant plastic playhouse. The pink-and-purple monstrosity stood out like a sore thumb in this quaint backyard.

"Hello!" Autumn called as she let herself in the gate.

The girls scrambled over to their aunt for a quick hug before racing back to their playhouse.

Autumn grabbed a plastic chair from the stack and settled next to Laney. "What's that smile for?"

Her friend was right—she was smiling. Thinking about Ethan did that to her. "Just happy."

"Wouldn't have anything to do with my brother, would it?"

Heat rose in her cheeks. "Maybe."

"Tell me." The girls chattered away, clearly not listening in.

"Oh, where to start?" Laney mused. "He is nothing like this guy I dated a few years ago. I thought he was a good guy. But after a few months, I discovered he was married. With children." She blew out her frustration. "He played me like a fool, and it kind of wounded me."

"Oh, my, what a lying cheater he was. You deserve so much better." Autumn's gaze held a protective glint Laney appreciated. "Ethan's a great guy."

"Says his sister." They both laughed.

Yesterday afternoon, she and Ethan had gone to the hardware store. He had placed his hand on the small of her back as they walked from one sample countertop to the next, and it had felt right.

She spent so much time with him that her attraction had grown with each passing day. She attempted to push her feelings away, but so far hadn't been successful. And the twins. They perched on the top of their playhouse, pretending it was a ship—how creative and adorable. What would she do without them in a few weeks?

"Sounds like you're growing closer."

"Yes. But we're just friends." She tried to tell herself that every night when she laid her head on the pillow and Ethan's face popped into her mind. Nightly, she second-guessed her decision to trade services because she could tell she was falling for the man and she didn't want to. Whatever was happening between them scared her.

She had to remain focused on her goal: her successful wedding venue. So she could not get sidetracked by a man.

"It was good to see you at the women's Bible study last night."

"I know." She peeked at the girls. "Everyone is just so friendly here."

"Speaking of friendly, any decisions on renewing the lease?" Autumn wiggled her eyebrows.

She groaned. The McCaws had been so good to her, and her aunt and uncle, over the years. "I want to figure out a compromise that won't disturb the pastureland too much."

"I'm glad to hear that. We all are." Just then, Autumn's phone rang. After listening for a few moments, her facial expression went from peaceful to worried. She stood. "I'll be right there." After she hung up, she said, "Sorry, gotta go." Then she hurried out of the yard.

With her thumb stuck in her mouth, Tori toddled over, climbed into Laney's lap and curled up like a little puppy. Her big eyes looked up at Laney with such trust.

"Tired?" Laney pushed the little girl's hair

from her damp face. She didn't dare ask if they wanted to go inside. If she'd learned one thing from watching these children for nearly two weeks, it was to not give them options. The adult made the choices and persuaded the children to accept them.

Tori shook her head, then placed her palms against Laney's cheek, her fingers sticky against Laney's skin. "Will you be my mommy?"

Laney's heart came to a stop. *Mommy?* Yes, she cared for the girls—and Ethan—but marriage and motherhood? She didn't think so.

"Maddy has a mommy." Tori crammed her thumb back into her mouth. "I want one, too."

Her heart broke for these children to be without a mother. "Even though I'm only your nanny, I love you, sweetheart." Laney wrapped her arms around Tori.

"No. I want a *mommy*. You're only a morning mommy. Maddy's mommy lives with her all the time."

That sounded wonderful. But she and Ethan weren't looking for a relationship of any kind. Laney kissed Tori's temple. She savored the moment and took note of her peace and contentment for when she wouldn't get to see them every day or spend hours playing with them. Before long, Tori spotted her sister in the sandbox and took off to join her. Though rambunctious and sneaky, they were also loving and well-behaved—when they wanted to be.

She peeked at her phone. Ethan should be home any minute. Cardinal wings beat against her chest at the thought of his arrival.

Stop, she chided herself. She was just the nanny. The arrangement would be over in a little more than four weeks. Her thoughts and heart charged way too far ahead.

"Water?" Tori skipped from the sandbox and held out her drink.

Laney reached for Tori's purple sippy cup. Empty. "Let me go fill this for you, honey." She grabbed Zoe's pink one as well, then slipped through the slider and moved to the kitchen to fill the cups. So much had changed in a week, the girls now acted well-behaved and listened to her. If she had a free hand, she'd give herself a congratulatory pat on the back.

When she stepped onto the patio, the girls were no longer in sight. Her throat tightened. She glanced all over the backyard and into the fields beyond. They weren't here. She had stepped away for only a couple of moments. *Where'd they go?*

"Tori? Zoe? Come out." Her gaze darted around the empty yard. "You're scaring me."

Cora and Wade's pool! Neither girl knew how to swim. She sprinted across the backyard, through the gate, crossed the high grasses between the houses and peeked over the pool fence. Empty.

She stilled.

The chicken coop! She bolted over, but only clucking hens greeted her.

The sound of her heartbeat raced in her ears. On her return, she called their names as loud as she could. Sweat dripped down her face. She searched the entire backyard. Rushed into the house and checked each room. No Tori. No Zoe.

She should have known watching kids couldn't be this easy. Why had she assumed things were going so well?

She ran into the backyard, looking for the girls. Where had they gone?

Worry churned her gut. Somehow, she had put the twins in danger.

Clearly Tori had chosen the wrong person to want as a mother.

Ethan strode to the little cul-de-sac his parents had added when he graduated high school. With six home lots carved out, one held the big ranch house, another Ethan's little bungalow, and four were still wooded parcels. His mom and dad had hoped that each of their children would build a home on the family ranch. So far, just him.

As he approached his home, he remembered Laney settling on the floor with the girls this morning and helping them with their new chunky puzzles. It looked like she fit right into his home. Almost like she belonged.

He spotted Laney around the side of the house. She wore a modest white T-shirt, light gray cropped pants and flip-flops. Her wavy hair bounced around her face as she moved.

"Zoe! Tori!" Laney called out, her voice frantic.

Ethan rushed to the backyard. "What's going on?" He rounded the corner of the house, gaze darting around the yard.

"I went inside to fill their sippy cups." Her voice came out in spurts. "When I came back two minutes later, they were gone. Just disappeared. They're not at the pool or the chicken coop."

As soon as Laney's shaky voice told him the twins were missing, Ethan knew exactly where they were. He took Laney's hand in his. "I think I know where they are."

"You do?" she squeaked. This morning, some

of her hair had been pulled back with a barrette, but now wisps framed her worried face.

Their fingers touched at the exchange. Interest zinged at her soft fingers resting in his hand. He shook the feeling away and tried to ignore the attraction bubbling between them.

"I know they're curious and busy, but they hide under the willow tree a lot. I probably should have mentioned it to you."

She wrapped her palm around his upper arm. "I hope they're there, because I can't find them anywhere." She squeezed his arm so hard it almost hurt.

They stepped to the edge of the property where the large willow tree stood. As they approached, he spotted the twins' silhouettes mingled with the tree limbs. He swept back the branches to reveal his giggling girls.

"No, Daddy, you didn't say 'ready or not, here I come,'" Zoe stated, a stern look on her face.

He released the branches to cover them again as Laney loosened her grip on his arm and murmured her thanks. Relief shone in her eyes.

He loved how she cared so deeply for his family.

"Ready or not, here I come," he announced, then moved the branches.

"You found us!" Zoe grinned.

When both girls looked up at him, he saw Joy's eyes. His throat constricted at the thought of his ex-wife.

He dropped Laney's hand. Would she leave, just like Joy had? Why did it matter to him, as long as she stayed for the six weeks she promised?

The hair on the back of his neck rose with his crystallized realization—Laney had turned into more than a nanny to him.

Push away these feelings, man.

The kids took off running after each other. He reveled in their playfulness.

"I'm so sorry about losing them." Laney's face held concern. "And here I thought I was doing such a good job. Had everything under control."

He chuckled. "Toddler twins are like treading water. Don't worry about it—I take full responsibility. I don't think I added hiding under the willow tree to the book." Though he wasn't sure she had spent a lick of time looking at the reference guide. Instead, she'd chosen to get to know his girls on her own, which was probably even better.

Loving his children was the quickest way to his heart. Except the last thing he wanted was to fall in love again.

"I have lunch ready."

"You didn't have to do that, though I'm thrilled you did. How about we let them get their energy out? Nap time will work better that way."

His productive and rewarding morning flitted through his mind. Without Laney's land, their daily ranching life would change. "Have you thought any more about the lease?"

"I found several ceremony locations. I can't decide on which to use." She worried her bottom lip. "Maybe I'll use them all. Brides love choices."

He could kick himself for not agreeing to Arthur subdividing the land and getting the purchase taken care of ten years ago. But he'd barely been in his twenties and hadn't really been making business decisions back then. His dad always said that monthly payments seemed easier than taking on more debt. Though, if Ethan had purchased the land, then he and Laney would be having a different conversation. Perhaps even more intense, because Laney had always assumed all of Arthur's land would be hers.

"I'd be happy to look at the locations and give my input." He kept his tone neutral, trying not to scare her off. He could give his honest opinion and at the same time encourage her to renew the lease.

"I'd like that. Every time I ask Autumn to help, she toes the party line that the McCaw cattle need the land."

While he respected how Laney stood up for herself, he'd do his best to give her the most neutral advice possible. He focused on the girls chasing each other. "My dad is meeting with an adjacent rancher tonight to see if we can lease from him."

"I'm still hoping we can figure out a way to share." She hugged her middle.

"Seems the income would help your wedding venue." Did a light flicker in her eyes? He hoped his family could continue to lease from her. And maybe... He shook the thought away, refusing to think about the possibility of a relationship.

"How was your day?" When she was uncomfortable, she switched the topic.

He smiled. "Very good. Thanks for bringing the twins to the pasture earlier. It was nice to get a Tori and Zoe fix midmorning." Carter, his brother, had commented that Ethan could not seem to stop smiling. Something about how much Laney cared about his twins had gotten into his heart.

"They seemed a little tired, so I put them in their stroller without a plan." A rush of color hit her cheeks. "Anyway, it was cool to see you in your element. You are such a cowboy at heart. You seem like you love your job."

It was nice that a city gal respected him as a rancher. Joy never had. She'd always told him that ranching and the ranch life were beneath her. "I'm fortunate in that regard." He cocked his head. "How did you know where I was this morning?"

"Oh, I spotted the board in the upper barn when I was wandering around over the weekend." Her eyes crinkled. "I can't tell you how much we discussed them staying in the stroller. If they even touched their buckles, I was going to turn around and leave."

Ethan laughed. "Yup. From birth, I've worked on them respecting cows and horses. Right now, they move too quick for most livestock, so I'm afraid they'd get hurt, and frankly, it wouldn't be the fault of the animal."

"You've done such a good job parenting."

His cheeks heated as the girls ran to him and each grabbed one of his legs.

The verse he'd read this morning from Jeremiah came to mind again. The Lord was comforting him from the wounds of the past.

His mother had recently told him she was thankful Joy made a clean break with them. Otherwise, the girls would be caught in a tug-of-war. Now the girls had stability. And they had a strong father, an aunt and uncles, and a grandmother and grandfather who adored and loved them.

Yes, the marriage was hard. The breakup was even more so. But if not for the hard time, he wouldn't have his girls.

"We wanna go in," they whined.

He walked toward the sliding door, the girls holding on to his legs to get a ride to the house. The patio had chalk strewn over it, along with lots of drawings. "Look at the pretty pictures."

The girls immediately jumped off. "We signed them—see?"

Sure enough, he spied a big, unsteady *T* and *Z* under two drawings. "Did you hold their hands and help?" he asked Laney.

"Nope. They did it all by themselves."

He was surprised, as he quickly calculated their age against a milestone chart he'd recently seen. "You taught them how to write letters?" He turned his attention to the twins. "You signed those masterpieces all by yourself?" He blinked away the sudden moisture and hugged them. "I'm so proud of both of you." With his phone, he snapped a quick series of pictures so they'd be able to remember the first time they wrote a letter.

Laney opened the door, and they all went in. She bustled to the kitchen and served four healthy lunch plates of turkey roll-ups, fresh fruit and what tasted like his mother's banana bread.

His heart swelled at her thoughtfulness. The twins needed—no, deserved—a mother. And his feelings toward Laney were growing stronger and stronger.

He recalled the warmth of her hand in his. He wasn't an affectionate person, yet her touch sparked something deep inside.

But that was no reason to encourage a relationship between them.

Nope. If they tried and it didn't work, she'd leave a hole in his life.

And he wasn't sure he could live through that again.

Chapter Eight

Saturday morning, when Laney spotted Ethan in her driveway helping the twins out of their car seats, her hope for a productive day vanished. "I thought your mom was watching them today." Tori and Zoe gave her a quick hug and then took off into the barn to investigate.

"Dad fainted this morning." He rubbed the scruff of his neck. "Probably just low blood sugar combined with low blood pressure, but Mom thought it'd be best if he had a quiet day."

"Oh, my. Hope he can rest." She furrowed her brow. Since the precocious girls were a handful, she and Ethan wouldn't be able to focus on anything other than watching the twins. Goodness, two days ago she had lost them—well, they'd been hiding beneath the willow tree, but still.

Her mind raced. What could they do around the house today and still be effective?

She spotted the bandage on Tori's elbow, covering the mark from when she fell on the patio yesterday. "I feel so bad about Tori falling."

"It wasn't your fault she was rushing and slipped. And it's healing very nicely." His eyes shone with gratitude, probably that she had made it to the two-week mark of babysitting the twins.

He was such a good father and she really enjoyed watching his children, maybe more than she should.

Through the kicked-up dust from Ethan's vehicle, her contractor's truck appeared. Ethan moved beside her.

Steve parked and trudged over to them. "Laney, we have a minor problem." His face was drawn.

Her chest tightened. Oh, no. The project had been growing each time she met with her contractor. More time. More money. What now? Ethan's fingers fluttered against hers, a reminder she wasn't in this alone.

"We ran into an issue with the city. Turns out we'll need a larger septic tank, along with a bigger leach field. When they came out to permit the bridal suite, I told them about the plans for the two additional bathrooms near the reception hall." He shrugged. "They calculate usage on worst-case scenarios. So if you have a hundred guests here for four hours, that's the formula they use for septic and leach field requirements. I think you were looking at only a hundred guests?"

She gulped, nodding.

He told her the estimate he'd worked up for the additional work.

Her breath hitched, and the air disappeared from her lungs. This entire project was based on a spreadsheet her friend Rose, the financial planner, had helped build. There was no line item for this extra work, nor the cost of her longed-for walkway to at least one ceremony location, which she had to include. This and the galvanized pipe fix made her way over budget, and the job had just started.

Her plan of doing a bunch of easier tasks, purchasing only thrift-sale items to outfit the spaces, and using lower-end finishes that looked higher-end, would no longer help her stay on budget.

She'd have to call Rose and figure out if maybe it made sense for Laney to pick up extra website design work to pay for these additional expenses.

Because a larger loan was out of the question.

Bad news delivered, Steve drove away, his dented truck disappearing in a cloud of dust—along with any possibility of opening in early fall like she had dreamed. "What am I going to do?"

"I could dig the new septic tank hole. Triple C has an excavator, and I know how to use it."

Hope vibrated in her core. "Could you?"

Ethan bumped her shoulder and tossed her a grin. Heat flamed her cheeks.

"Of course. I love playing on the excavator." His eyes sparkled.

Though, excitement soon gave way to trepidation as the location of the future ceremonies swirled around in her mind. Yesterday, when she and Autumn had driven around the property, her friend had expressed concern about the family's ranching needs and how Laney's ideas would put a big dent in their operations.

Maybe Autumn was wrong? Perhaps when Ethan heard her plans, he'd be encouraging.

Either way, she wanted to get her mind off Steve's bad news. "Let me show you my ceremony location spots. We can take the UTV."

Ethan corralled the girls, and they loaded up. At the last moment, Ace jumped on the back and pushed his head between the twins.

Laney pressed the gas, and they were on their way, the warm breeze blowing her hair back. She smiled, remembering the times she galloped horses as a teen. Where had her playful nature gone?

When she stopped, Ace jumped off and barked a few times. They were close to the bluff overlooking the creek. "Can you two stay here for just a minute?" At the twins' dual nods, she grabbed Ethan's hand and pulled him along to the edge. Her pulse fluttered at his rough cowboy skin against hers. "Isn't this a gorgeous setting?"

The creek rippled below them, natural shrubs lined up along the water as though vying for a drink.

She grinned. "This is it. Or at least this is one of the location finalists." She turned to face the pasture, dropped his hand and released a nervous breath.

She recalled a week ago, when the toy store employee thought she was the girls' mother. A warmth had grown inside her chest and hadn't left. Perhaps all nannies adored their charges, but the family feeling she'd felt since that day did nothing but build with each passing day.

She did her best to focus on the moment at hand. "A trellis right here, a short stone wall along the edge to prevent any mishaps. Do you see it?"

"I've always loved this spot." Ethan's lips were pursed together. Had she irritated him? Surely this tiny square of land wouldn't affect his cattle grazing.

She shook off the notion as excitement bubbled inside. She wrapped her hand around his upper arm and squeezed. "The couple could get married here at sunset. The view, the creek gurgling, string lights for ambience." She released his arm and sighed. She could get used to this.

Fields dotted with mooing cows stood before her. The girls had scrambled off the vehicle and were chasing each other around it.

"Come on—there's more." Enthusiasm laced her tone as she jogged back to the UTV, Ace right behind her.

Once everyone was in safely, they lurched forward and started on their way.

She worried her bottom lip. "Let me show you the other location I'm thinking of." Before the kids tried to get out, she drove them to the edge of the pond surrounded by trees and parked. Cows stood at the water's edge and drank. "Isn't it beautiful?"

He jumped out and pointed, his features tense. "Laney, several of our pastures feed into

this reservoir for the cattle to drink fresh water."
His shoulders slumped.

Her zeal for the pond—with the hills mounding in the background as a secondary ceremony location—immediately fell.

She hadn't considered that this was a natural water source for him. This moment probably wasn't the best time to bring up her ingenious shared-use idea, based on day of the week. Because now that she thought about it, he'd likely disagree with her brilliance. He was in a bad mood right now, and she didn't want to freak him out even more.

Except that cow getting loose and eating her petunias was a problem. Yes, Colt had corralled the animal quickly that day, but what if there were no cowboys around to help? Cows kept escaping and ended up grazing in her front yard. One even stole Ace's metal water bowl and carried it around with him like a toy. And she tried to forget about the day when a dozen from the herd had shown up. Not good at all.

She kicked at grass along the edge of the picturesque pond. "I'm still concerned about the cattle escaping and joining a wedding reception. Something like that might just tank my new business."

His face tightened. "Really? I mean, you're

offering a rustic wedding experience to your clients. What would it matter if a cow stumbled in by accident?"

She blinked, her irritation rising. "You don't understand at all. A cow would ruin the special day in an instant."

Why didn't Ethan understand everything needed to be perfect? If a cow made an appearance and she received negative reviews, her venue would go under quickly.

"Yes, I do. You're bringing in city people to get a taste of the country. No city person would bat an eye at a cow showing up. They might even think you planned it."

She rolled her eyes. "You've got to be kidding. Open spaces, nature noises—that's what they're paying for. That's what they expect. Not cows bullying their way in."

"Laney, our lease ends in a few weeks. If we need to find land elsewhere, you'll need to give us time to prep the land."

Every time the lease renewal surfaced, his crushed expression reminded her of his promise to his late grandfather.

"Don't rush me," she said angrily, putting some distance between her and his desire to monopolize her land.

"Listen, I thought we had a backup plan with

the Millers, but I found out yesterday they sold their land to a rancher moving here from Arizona." He huffed out a breath. "Our only other option would be more than a couple of miles away, making day-to-day operations much more difficult, maybe even impossible." His eyes pleaded with her.

She swallowed and focused on the still pond. "I'm sorry, but I can't decide until I'm sure the plan we agree upon will work for my wedding venue." She turned to him and blew a lock of hair away from her face.

"Well, we need to know sooner rather than later, Laney. We can't grow grass on another stretch of land in the blink of an eye." His face hardened.

"And I can't decide overnight," she snapped.

She couldn't decide right now. Not yet.

Was her indecision because she wanted the McCaws to end up happy, or was it wound up in something else?

"Ethan, if we can't work out a compromise, you can use the pastures for a few more months, or whatever you need, while you make other arrangements."

Relief crossed his features. "Thank you, Laney. We appreciate that."

A cow snort startled her. She jumped. Where

had that Angus come from? He pushed his black head toward her, lightly touching her and causing her to lose her balance.

"See, this is exactly the problem. Not only do they get out of the fencing, but they think they are part of the family," she huffed. "What normal cow wants to be petted?"

She stepped away and smoothed her Bermuda shorts. Maybe that was her problem. Maybe she was trying so hard to be included with the McCaws that it petrified her to disappoint them.

She was a businessperson. She had to do what was best for her wedding venue. Period.

But the more time she spent in Serenity, the more she realized that business and personal had more of an overlap than they did in San Antonio. Here there were many shades of gray.

How was she ever going to figure out the perfect solution for her venue and the Triple C, and feel peace about her decision?

Ethan's body tensed. With the Millers selling, this land was his only hope. If they didn't renew the lease with Laney, they might go under. And then his promise to his grandfather would be broken. What would happen to the McCaw family if the Triple C went bankrupt?

He shifted his hat to shield the June sun while the girls giggled and frolicked in the pastures. Carefree.

Envy crawled up his spine. How he longed for life to return to normal, before Laney had shown up and jeopardized his livelihood and the family business.

He wanted to hop off the vehicle and march back to the safe haven of his truck, but he restrained himself. Yes, he wanted her venue to succeed, but didn't she understand she likely wouldn't use a significant amount of their leased land? He wished she'd just renew their lease and be done with it. They could work out the fine details later, but he was thankful she'd at least allow them to keep using her land while they prepped pastures elsewhere.

His father's words from last night floated into his head: *If Laney doesn't renew the lease, we'll work it out. Somehow, God will provide.*

But trusting and not relying on others was still a struggle for Ethan. He even continued to wrestle with trying to make his parents proud. Make sure they weren't second-guessing adopting him. Investing in him.

Just then, his phone chimed. Joy. Sorry about yesterday, the evening got away from me. How are the twins?

The text ended with heart and hug emojis. He pocketed his phone, pushed Joy from his mind and tried to come up with some alternative plan that didn't run the Triple C out of business.

"Joy?"

He cocked his head. "How'd you know?"

"You get a look about you when she texts. I remember the text she sent when I first arrived and we were at Pops in the Park." She worried her hands. "Feel free to reply."

"No. It's not important." He wasn't sure how he felt about Laney being able to see through him so easily.

"I've never seen her around town." Though her ponytail had gotten messier each time they drove around the pastures on the UTV, it was just as attractive as when she styled it for Pops in the Park or dinners at the big house.

"She lives in Dallas. I think." He rubbed the scruff of his neck. "She texts on Friday nights to check in. I think it makes her feel good about herself."

Zoe raced toward them. "I need to use the potty, Daddy." A look of distress came across her face as she squished her knees together.

"Me, too. Me, too." Tori ran over to join her twin.

Ethan and Laney shared a knowing glance.

They had been working on potty training the past few weeks.

"We're closer to my house than yours." He pointed toward the McCaw spread. "I'll show you the way."

He slid into the passenger seat and helped the girls onto the bench seat. With only a few weeks left on their land lease, Ethan's nerves were frayed.

Laney whistled, and Ace jumped onto the back seat, resting his paws between them like he'd done each time they'd gotten in the UTV.

As Laney headed toward his house, Ethan wrapped his arm around the twins to stabilize them. She parked in the shade just beyond his white picket fence.

He stepped off, but the girls insisted they didn't need any help and ran into the house alone.

As he scooted back on the seat, the scent of wildflowers filled his senses.

"Sorry about earlier," she said softly. "I'm just having a difficult time wrapping my head around the land and how we can share it." She settled her palm on his upper arm. "Ethan, please know that I want to honor Arthur's promise."

He blew out a relieved breath. Could she be closer to signing than he'd expected?

Fallen blond strands curved around her face, her messy ponytail appearing as though it could come undone with the next swift breeze. She looked up at him with such tenderness.

His gut coiled into a tight knot. What was happening? Was he falling for Laney? No, it couldn't be. That didn't fit in with his plans.

"We done." Zoe raced toward them, wiping her palms on the pretty dress she'd insisted on wearing.

"We washed." Tori lifted her dripping hands as she followed her sister.

Zoe startled and pointed at the garden. "Peas, Daddy?"

"No," he said.

"Sure," Laney stated at the exact moment.

He glared at her.

The twins scrambled into the garden, homing in on their favorite raw vegetable. Tori and Zoe pulled the pods open and chomped on the peas. Dressed in coordinating pastels, they looked like catalog models posing in front of the deep green shrubbery that hid the gated pool and his parents' ranch house.

He shook his head. "You need to learn when to say no to them." Laney had a penchant for letting the girls steamroll over her.

"What?"

"There's two of them. And only one of you. It's easy to lose control."

Her face squished up. "Lose control? Do you have a problem with how I am caring for your kids?"

"No, no, not at all." Ugh, his choice of words couldn't have been worse.

A splash sounded. His stomach dropped.

Zoe. Tori. He jerked his head. They were no longer in the garden. He dashed through the vegetable rows and around the hedge. The pool gate stood wide-open. He rushed through.

Tori, in the shallow end, had taken off her sandals and happily kicked the water with her bare feet. Zoe was standing on the diving board!

"Zoe! No!"

Their gazes snagged. Fear registered on her face. She turned, lost her balance and tumbled into the pool. He dived in after her. When they surfaced, her eyes were wide.

He struggled out of the pool, his now-wet jeans weighing a ton. Water dripped from Zoe's soaking clothes.

She whimpered as her eyes filled with tears. "Daddy. Daddy." Her lower lip trembled.

He squeezed her tighter and pressed a kiss to her damp forehead.

"Zoe, you okay?" Tori joined them, petting her sister like a dog.

The sound of Ethan's heartbeat thrashed in his ears as he rocked back on his heels.

He closed his eyes, vowing to teach them how to swim. Soon. Reaching down, he scooped up Tori, hugging her tight. The open gate mocked him. Who had left it wide-open?

"Is everyone okay?" Laney rushed over.

Tori's bottom lip puckered out. "Zoe fell in the pool." Fat tears slipped down her cheeks as she leaned into Laney.

Laney comforted Tori, allowing her pretty clothes to get wet. She was a good mother figure for the girls and he never should have doubted her earlier.

She tossed him a worried look.

His knees wobbled at her love and concern for the twins. It was one thing to have the girls in danger, but his heart?

He gave her a shaky smile and squeezed Zoe closer.

He wanted to turn and run, but something held him here. If he were honest with himself, he was interested to see what might happen between them.

He'd become attached to Laney. Being with her simply felt right.

In high school, she had been way too young for him. Now? Well, at their age, four years didn't mean too much.

Was he ready to dive into a relationship knowing he, and the girls, could get hurt all over again?

Chapter Nine

A week later, her contractor, Steve, stopped Laney as she stepped into Mabel's Diner to meet Autumn for Sunday lunch. When she saw his tense face, her mood shifted to worry about what additional problems he had for her today.

Classical music was coming from speakers in the corners of the restaurant, but she could barely hear it through the din of customers chatting and silverware clanking.

"I have the estimate for the paved walkway to the bluff." Steve frowned.

Oh, no. She rubbed her suddenly damp palms on her floral dress.

"Like we talked about earlier in the week, the bluff is about half a mile from the barn." He then named a price she couldn't afford.

She dropped her gaze to the worn black-and-white-checked linoleum floor. The walkway would tie everything together, kind of like a ribbon on a wrapped gift. How could she open a wedding venue without it?

"Then I'm not sure I can afford paved." The sour taste of failure filled her. How could she have a successful wedding venue without access to the ceremony locations? And if this path was expensive, a path to the more remote pond was out of the question. "And I can't have gravel." She huffed.

"Why not?"

"Women can't walk on gravel in heels."

He looked at her like she was nuts. And maybe she was.

Her stomach churned. What would she do? All the guests couldn't be transported on a UTV—that would be a logistics nightmare. She required a pathway on which guests could walk on their own. Otherwise, she'd be forced to offer the backyard as the ceremony spot. And that wouldn't do.

"Listen, Steve, thanks for looking into this for me. Let me think about it and get back to you." Her jaw shifted. Who was she kidding? This entire project was careening out of control.

As Steve went over to join his family, Autumn entered the diner and gave Laney a much-needed hug.

Before they could seat themselves, Mabel appeared and wrapped her arms around Laney. "So good to see you, sweetie. And before you ask, everything is set for the anniversary party." She released her hold and stepped back. "Now sit down and get yourself a proper meal." She looked Laney up and down. "You could use some meat on those bones."

She and Autumn settled and perused the menus. "Ignore her," Autumn said. "I think you look great."

"Thanks," Laney stated as Mabel came back with a pot of coffee for the table and fresh cream. She poured them each a cup. Laney doctored hers up. People crowded the diner, likely lunching after the church service. Little had changed since she'd last been in Serenity.

"What's wrong?" Autumn leaned back, probably waiting to hear an explanation for the gloomy look on Laney's face.

Her stomach growled at the delicious breakfast smells in the diner while she shared the estimate Steve had given her and then stressed the importance of the path.

Autumn shrugged. "It's one of those necessary expenses. Can't you get a larger loan?"

"I don't want to," she said. "My mother stole my identity when I was eighteen and ruined my credit."

Autumn sucked in a breath. "No way."

"Yup. Rose, my friend that I've told you about, helped me work with the credit card company to pay back my mother's debt. It took three years. I'm super careful with finances now."

"I'm sorry that happened to you." Autumn tapped her index finger against her chin. Her eyes lit up. "How about doing a gravel path instead? If your customers are looking for an authentic cowboy wedding, give it to them."

"But women in heels…"

She cocked her head. "Everyone should wear cowboy attire."

Hope expanded Laney's chest. She'd been trying to put her new business in a box, seeking to replicate other wedding venues she had read about. But her location was unique. She'd be giving clients an experience. "You're right. And the path could be more narrow—I bet that would lower the cost. I'll look into it. Thanks." Maybe Autumn's idea would work.

She stirred her coffee. "I noticed Ethan and the girls weren't at church this morning. Is everything okay?" Laney went for a nonchalant tone. She didn't want Autumn picking up on her attraction to Ethan.

In the past few weeks their friendship had bloomed. It was exciting and scary at the same time. They'd both been hurt in the past and neither one of them was looking for a relationship, but something drew them to each other.

At each Pops in the Park she'd attended, they'd ended up together, strolling on the brick path through the town square, chatting about…everything. Sundays after church, except this morning, they'd let the girls play on the playground near the nursery while they talked. This past week, Cora and Wade had watched television at his house so he could come over after putting the girls down for bed. Some nights she and Ethan did little construction projects. Other evenings they sat on the porch swing and talked of their dreams and past hardships. As they grew closer, fear and excitement vied for her attention.

"Zoe isn't feeling well," Autumn told her as she sipped her coffee.

Laney immediately whipped out her phone and shot a text to Ethan. I heard Zoe is sick. Is she okay? Need help? She hit Send before allowing herself to second-guess. And impatiently waited for a reply before allowing worry to settle in.

Four weeks. She'd only been here four short weeks, and already those girls—and Ethan, if she were honest—meant a lot to her. He was a loving father and had created a warm and inviting home to raise his children in. Maybe she'd gotten ahead of herself. Maybe she'd fallen for all the things that Ethan was instead of the actual man.

"What'd you think of the service this morning?" Autumn asked.

"Powerful. I wasted so many years in San Antonio, thinking that moving back here would label me a failure. But here I am."

"I'm thrilled you're back." She leaned forward, eyes sparkling. "Seems like you might have a crush on my big brother."

"No." She quickly rejected Autumn's assessment. "Ethan's just such a great father and, I don't know, a genuine cowboy."

"Like I said. Sounds like a crush."

Feeling her cheeks grow hot from blushing, she tried to change the subject. "How's the guest list coming for the anniversary party?"

Autumn pressed her hands together. "Okay. So this might be a little over-the-top, but I want to invite all the residents of Serenity."

"That's great, so great. Cora will love it and Wade will be embarrassed, but in the end it'll be a ton of fun." She sipped her coffee. "Did your brother book the trio?"

"Yes, Walker did." Her face fell, like every time Walker came up in conversation. "I'm worried about him."

Her youngest brother was a security specialist who worked for some high-tech company but lived right here in Serenity. Something tragic had happened to his wife, and Walker seemed emotionally scarred. Poor guy.

"I know you're close to him."

She nodded. "So, you don't think inviting everyone will be too over-the-top?"

"It's sweet, Autumn. Your parents will love it. But I'll have to alert the food vendors. It might cost a little more."

"They're worth it. So, what's happening with food?"

Before Laney had a chance to reply, the waitress came and took their order. An omelet and fruit for Autumn. French toast for Laney.

Laney then gave her an update on refreshments for the party. All five restaurants in town were taking part. "I even got the church to agree to bring tables for the food and scatter chairs around so people can sit while they eat. Also, Lily is selling us last season's party supplies at cost."

Autumn clapped at the party store owner's generosity while Laney tried to let the kindness of everyone in this town sink in. Serenity was a true community. You could count on these people in good and bad times.

"You are a party whisperer."

Laney waved her friend off. "It was easy, because everyone is so giving and kind."

"So are you. You know, I think Ethan might be the one." Autumn's now-soft voice forced Laney to lean forward. "And I know he likes you. A lot. He's never acted this way before. Not even with Joy."

Could it be true? Could Ethan care for her as more than a friend—more than a nanny?

Would she be willing to risk leaning on a man? She tamped down her anxiety as the waitress dropped off the food and refilled their coffee. Laney thanked her and stirred cream into her steaming drink.

"You deserve your white-picket-fence dream, Laney. You just need to learn to trust." Autumn's eyes pierced hers and warmed her heart.

She was right. Because of her mother, she had made every adult decision out of fear. Could she learn to step out in faith and rely on other people?

Maybe it was a sign that Ethan's home was ensconced behind a white picket fence.

Being around him every day was getting more and more difficult. She had already fallen head over heels for the twins, and now she was doing the one thing she had promised she'd never do: considering a relationship, maybe even long term. But she wasn't there yet.

Her phone dinged. I didn't want to bother you on your day off.

Her insides vibrated, alarming Laney. She wasn't sure she was ready to open herself up to anyone. But she had to find out if Zoe was okay. Don't be silly. How's Zoe doing?

Still has a fever. Now Tori does as well.

Anything I can do for you?

No, Zoe has been asking for you, but she'll see you tomorrow, assuming their fevers are gone.

I can stop by on my way back.

Would you mind?

Laney gathered up her things and put a ten-dollar bill in the middle of the table, leaving most of her food uneaten. She was no longer hungry. "Something's come up. Call you later?" She ignored the surprise in her friend's eyes.

It was about time to allow herself to go after her dream of a family. A real home.

"Tell Ethan I said hi," Autumn called after her.

Of course, her friend guessed why she had departed so quickly.

She had to get over to Ethan's as soon as possible or her chest would explode. Zoe had asked for her.

Ethan's comment last weekend—*you need to learn when to say no to the girls*—still gnawed at her. She could refuse the girls' requests—she could. But if she were honest with herself, he was right. The twins had her wrapped around their pinkies and refusing them was a challenge.

She rushed to her car. Truth was, she couldn't wait to see Ethan. Spend time with him. Talk with him.

Somehow he'd become very important to her. What if she fell for him completely?

But to allow her dream to happen, she'd have to put her fears aside.

As she started her car, something beneath her ribs pounded. If she put herself out there, could a relationship between them bloom?

* * *

He had been cooped up in the house with his twins for over twenty-four sleepless hours. Not that Ethan was complaining. But with fevers, they were ornery. After a call to the pediatrician last night, Ethan was convinced they both had a cold, since their fevers weren't too high. If the doctor wasn't worried, Ethan tried not to be.

He scanned the window overlooking his front yard. No Laney yet.

He missed their opportunity to chat while the girls played on the playground after church today. He had been enjoying their time together this past week. Each conversation they had seemed to draw them closer together. And he liked it.

With his free hand, he scraped his hair back as he continued to sway Tori from side to side in his arms. Why had he mentioned that Zoe had asked about her? He knew why. Because he wanted to see Laney.

His chest drummed in anticipation of her arrival. With all the time they'd been spending together, his feelings for Laney seemed to grow exponentially each day. A floorboard squeaked under his feet. He held his breath until he was sure the noise hadn't woken Tori.

He pressed his lips to Tori's forehead, and it seemed slightly cooler. Maybe. He shifted his sleepy toddler in his arms and continued rocking her.

When Laney finally rolled into his driveway, his heart knocked around like a herd of galloping horses. He shook his head. Lately, his emotions were up and down like a teenager's.

She opened the door and peeked in. "Can I come in?" she mouthed.

He nodded, trying to calm his heart rate. "I finally got Zoe asleep and put her in bed. So far, so good," he whispered.

Laney stopped, her blue dress flowing back and forth with every movement. "Oh, well, I don't want to wake her. Just tell her I dropped by." She turned.

"Wait," he said. Tori shifted at his urgent voice. "Please stay," he said softly.

Her tense shoulders seemed to relax as she closed the door, kicked her ivory heels off and walked over to him in bare feet. She gazed at Tori with love and worry, then leaned down and brushed her lips across his daughter's forehead.

Laney's wildflower perfume tickled his nose. The scent had once scared him—made him fear he'd care for someone and life would blow up again. Now he welcomed the smell. The feelings gave him hope. Maybe he was ready to move forward. Take a leap of faith.

"She feels pretty warm. I'm guessing she still has a fever," Laney whispered.

The compassionate words awoke something deep inside him. She cared deeply for his girls, and somehow, that bonded them.

If he wasn't careful, he might fall in love with Laney.

And he wasn't sure he wanted that to happen just yet.

"I take it Zoe calmed down Friday?" She gestured at the unicorn stuffed animal in the corner.

"Yes, she did. Her uncontrollable crying had nothing to do with you or the unicorn and everything to do with her exhaustion and that she was coming down with something." Laney's concern for his children delighted him.

From down the hall, Zoe began crying. "I'll get her." Laney moved swiftly and returned with Zoe in her arms. Laney dropped into the other rocker-recliner. She held Zoe tight to her body and rocked hard, just the way the girls liked it.

As he watched Laney hold his daughter, he yearned for a helpmate. Not just when they were sick, but to get them ready for school, to have meals with. He could see Laney being with the twins after they got off the school bus each day. Eating cookies, helping with homework and offering advice. She'd dole out biblical wisdom coupled with love.

"Her eyes are closing." Laney's husky voice was soft. Their gazes caught. Something passed between them.

"Thank you," he mouthed.

The room remained quiet for long moments, the rockers moving back and forth the only noise.

"I think Zoe is asleep." She rolled her forward so her face was visible.

"She is. Let's try putting them down." He rose, and Laney followed. Together, they gently laid each of the girls in their beds and covered them with their blankets. The moment felt downright homey, and he liked it.

Could he let himself trust another woman?

If the emotions that drew him to her like a magnet every time they were near had something to do with it, then this was love. But he wasn't sure she felt the same. Or that he even wanted to go down that road.

As a small-town cowboy, he was probably the last man she'd be interested in. Likely she was looking for someone more sophisticated.

He closed the door and followed Laney back to the living room. His growing feelings for Laney scared him. When Joy had left him and the girls, he thought he'd be single forever, destined to raise the twins on his own. Had Laney come into his life for a reason?

"I'm gonna get going," Laney stated.

"No." The word sounded harsh, but he wanted her to stay.

Surprise registered on her face.

"I meant, don't go. I'd love to continue our conversation." Maybe it was spending the last twenty-four hours alone with two sick toddlers, but he didn't want this time with Laney to end. Lately their goodbyes had become more and more difficult. "Can I get you something to eat?"

"Why don't we clean up these dishes before the girls wake?" She stood at the kitchen sink and began washing.

He took up the drying position. "By the way, thanks for watching the kids. They enjoy spending time with you so much, so I feel like I'm getting the better end of the bargain. It's always 'Laney this' and 'Laney that.'"

As she handed him a bowl, she gazed up at him. "Each week is better than the last. Once they got to know and trust me, they are really two little sweethearts. Not that we don't have our challenging moments." She chuckled.

He plunged forward. "I wanted to apologize for what I said last week." On the surface, everything had been fine between them. But he knew his statement about saying no to the girls had hurt Laney.

A bit of discomfort flashed across her face. "It's fine."

"No, it's not. I trust your judgment, Laney. I do."

Her face lit up. "Really?" She handed him a wet plate, and their fingers collided.

His breath caught. He nodded, afraid if he spoke, his voice would wobble.

"Oh, I saw my contractor at the diner earlier." She wiped her cheek with the back of her hand, her fingers dripping with soapy water. "I can't afford the wide paved walkway I had hoped for, so I'm going to change it to a much more narrow gravel path and simply let the brides know that everyone should dress for a rustic event." Her shoulders seemed to collapse as in defeat, but he was grateful for the compromise she chose.

It sounded as though she was one step closer to renewing their land lease. He wanted to dance around the kitchen, but he knew how crucial her wedding venue was to her. He hoped changing the path from paved to gravel wouldn't scare away clients, because he wanted her to succeed.

"And the pond?" He was almost afraid to ask.

"I can't afford it, not even close. Just the bluff. And I'll do something by the grove of trees in the backyard for an alternate ceremony location." She paused her washing to look at him. "The bluff shouldn't affect the pastures too much. Believe it or not, I want both businesses to thrive."

He released a ragged breath. Even though she hadn't said she'd renew their lease, given time, he could tell she would. "Thank you." He dried the dish and reached around her to put it away. The nearness almost made him dizzy. How would she react if he lifted her into his arms and twirled her around the tiny kitchen?

"You know, Ethan, I was thinking that, after painting the house, the barn looks dingy."

"Next weekend we'll paint it. I promise." The last weekend of June, he had planned for some townspeople to come help complete the barn. Empty it out, put a new structure in, complete the floor. He couldn't wait to see Laney's surprised face when they knocked on her door Saturday morning. By the end of that workday, they would transform the barn into a shabby-chic reception hall. Yes, Steve would still have work to do, but the transformation would have begun.

"Why don't we paint it tomorrow?" She raised her brows in hope. "Or at least get a start. I feel so behind on my to-do list. I mean, each time I cross off a task, I add three more things, and we haven't even started on the interior of the barn." Frustration laced her tone.

"We can't paint the barn—we need to power wash it first." Keeping this secret from Laney might be harder than he'd thought. He was nervous she'd find out about the workday before next Saturday, and he wanted to surprise her.

"You're right." She turned off the water, holding her dripping hands over the sink.

He offered her the damp towel. Miraculously, the girls remained asleep.

After she dried her hands, she smoothed her wavy hair. More than her looks, Ethan found her inner beauty attractive.

A vision of Joy came into his mind, but he shoved it away. Laney wasn't like Joy at all. The pull he felt toward Laney was something he had never felt before. Not even with Joy.

He wanted to try again. With Laney.

But did she care about him in the same way?

She had a heart for his daughters and an obvious love for his hometown. He dried and stowed the last plate. Being around Laney did something to him. Could he learn to trust again?

She reached for her water glass and finished drinking. He couldn't take his eyes off her. What would she think if he kissed her?

She set the glass down, and he leaned forward. Their gazes locked and their lips almost touched, but then a bloodcurdling cry emitted from the twins' bedroom.

He stepped back and hurried down the hall, rubbing a hand down his face.

The howl grew louder and more ominous.

Had he just been spared from making a huge mistake?

Chapter Ten

Early Saturday morning, Laney recalled the almost-kiss from a week ago. Maybe the moment had swept him up. Maybe he hadn't meant to lean in for a kiss. Maybe Zoe's distinctive cry had given him a way out.

Had she wanted him to kiss her? Yes. Definitely. And more than anything, that scared her. Either way, the week had been so busy they'd barely had any free time to spend together. Or maybe Ethan was avoiding her.

Ever since the debacle with her ex, Laney had promised herself to stay away from guys. And she had. Until Ethan. There was something special about him.

Except she feared her feelings for Ethan were too strong. Did she care for him more than he cared for her?

When a car horn beeped, she startled and coffee splashed from her mug onto the front of her white T-shirt. She rushed up to her bedroom and slipped on a clean shirt.

She opened the kitchen door, stepped onto the porch and came to an abrupt halt. Ethan, his siblings and a crew of townspeople stood there, grinning and holding power tools. What were all these people doing here?

Ethan perched on the bottom step. "Surprise!"

"What's going on?" She took a tentative step forward. Ace bulleted past her and ran to the welcoming clan, gathering rubs and caresses as he worked the crowd.

"It's a modern-day barn raising. Except we're going to renovate and paint the barn today. And a little more."

Tears threatened at Ethan's thoughtfulness and the time everyone standing here had given up, just to help her. Excitement ran through her at the possibility of completing some of the huge items on her to-do list, and maybe getting her budget back on track.

Her throat thickened at the expectation on Ethan's face. She threw her arms around him and squeezed tight. His powerful muscles flexed underneath her fingertips.

She might have clung too tight for too long, but she finally pulled away and drank in the crowd of people milling about.

As a hint of Ethan's spicy cologne clung to the air, bewilderment over this modern-day barn raising took hold. Otto from the ice cream store, with his adult sons. Theo from the Morning Grind. Steve, her contractor. Earl the veterinarian. She raced into Earl's arms.

"You all are so sweet." She pressed her face against Earl's wide chest.

He patted her back. "When Ethan put out the call, I just asked when. I'd do anything for you. Seems you'd have figured that out by now."

As she released the veterinarian, her heart overflowed and her eyes filled. Autumn stood between her brothers Carter, the ranch business manager, and Austin, who worked alongside Ethan on the ranch.

"I don't think you've met my brother Walker?" Autumn introduced the youngest McCaw, who owned a small house in town and worked remotely for a high-tech security firm headquartered in Dallas.

They shook hands. His eyes looked sad.

The whole time, Ethan remained by her side. He clapped his hands. "Okay, gather round, everyone." All the volunteers circled around and Ethan prayed for their productivity and safety.

Unshed tears skimmed her eyes. She didn't deserve all this kindness.

How had Ethan and the girls wormed their way into her heart so quickly? Normally, she didn't let people in so easily. She liked to guard her heart.

Steve handed out hard hats and goggles. "Laney, Ethan, what do you need everyone to do?"

Laney switched into work mode. "I need the extra items in the barn stacked on the porch. I'll have a garage sale or something for the bridles and saddles and anything else that's worth something."

Esther, Earl's wife, the owner of the local consignment store and leader of Laney's small group Bible study, stated she'd been looking for additional pieces to fill her tack section, and she'd love to buy the items outright. She named a more-than-generous price that would help Laney pay for some of the recent extra costs.

"Wow, Esther, are you sure?"

"Absolutely. I'll have the guys load what I want into my truck and the rest can go onto your porch. Does that sound good to you?"

"Oh, my, yes, it does. Thank you so much, Esther." She wrapped her arms around the older woman for a moment before Esther scurried off.

She turned to a younger group of helpers, who were waiting for instructions. When she told them they got to demo the tack room and horse stalls, they hooted their excitement.

"The whole barn needs to be painted." No wonder Ethan had insisted on the power wash earlier in the week and then put off the start of painting.

The workers milled about, accomplishing ten times what she and Ethan would have been able to get done today just the two of them.

It floored her that so many people would choose to help her on their Saturday. Was this how small towns were, or just Serenity? Either way, she was thankful her aunt and uncle had made this their home, and now she was doing the same.

Mabel, from the diner, and Opal, the receptionist from church, directed Otto and Theo in putting up a small white tent. Then they busied themselves setting up a table. A yellow basket with Clean written on the side was full of rags. A red basket had Used written on it. Then they set up two orange insulated beverage coolers, one with water, the other with sports drinks, and placed stacks of red plastic cups beside the drinks.

Not only did these sweet people show up, but they had arrived prepared.

She had a hard time grasping that Ethan had thought up this whole thing. For her.

"There you are." Ethan sidled up to her a while later and tossed her a lopsided grin. "I wanted to apologize for Zoe interrupting things…you know…the other day." He scrubbed a hand over his face.

Hope bloomed. He wasn't apologizing for the kiss; he was apologizing for the interruption.

"Can…can you see us together? Or am I really off base here?" His voice was low and deep.

Us. He thought there was an *us*? Her stomach flipped. She hadn't been sure. At a loss for words, she just nodded.

"I'm hoping sometime soon, the opportunity will present itself again." His gaze held hers.

Her pulse flickered at the hope of a future kiss.

He was unlike any other man she'd met. He wasn't trying to win her over—in fact, quite the opposite. Whatever was happening between them felt very natural.

He laced his fingers with hers and she rested her head on his shoulder. Soap mixed with hints of his distinctive aftershave tickled her nose. This felt like home.

Before long, Ethan was called away. He strode toward the old barn with purpose.

Workers buzzed about. She thanked them as they passed. Then she noticed a group of men around Ethan and unease gained a foothold.

Was the town supporting her or Ethan? If their relationship progressed and they started dating only to break up, would that ruin her chances of a successful business here?

Nagging doubt niggled at her brain. She had one shot at making this new business work, and she couldn't allow herself to be distracted.

Failure wasn't an option. If only she could manage her attraction to him as easily as coordinating a beautiful wedding.

The workers had demoed most of the stalls, and now they were moving debris into a dumpster. "Need help?" Ethan asked Earl.

"I think you'd do best overseeing, but thanks." Earl passed him with a cast-iron stall partition. They were collecting all the iron pieces in one area, since there was a profitable market in reselling them.

Ethan stepped aside. Autumn came alongside him and playfully bumped his shoulder. "This was a nice thing to do, brother."

He shrugged like it was nothing. "She's on a tight budget." He'd also wanted to see Laney's excitement when she spotted half the town in her front yard, eager to lend a helping hand. Her expression hadn't disappointed.

"I saw you holding Laney's hand earlier. Is she your girlfriend now?"

Even though he had hope, doubt plagued him. "No. I'm terrible at relationships—just ask Joy."

She cocked her head. "Joy? You take advice from an ex-wife who was horrible to you and didn't even want those sweet girls?" Irritation clung to her voice.

"Well, now hold on…"

"No. You don't get to say one nice thing about that woman. Not after she left you and the girls." Autumn pierced him with a look. "I follow her on social media, and I tell you, Joy goes through boyfriends faster than a runner goes through sneakers."

"What do you mean?"

"Seems like she always has a man by her side. Each one seems wealthier and more powerful than the last, as though she's working her way up the ladder."

For years now, he'd believed that he had been the root cause of their failed marriage.

Back when he'd informed his parents he and Joy were engaged to be married, his mother warned him that Joy appeared self-centered and she didn't believe Joy truly loved Serenity and ranching. His mother had speculated that Joy wanted way more than Ethan could ever provide. But, deeply in love, he hadn't listened to his mother's warnings.

"Joy told me that I was a horrible husband. Couldn't communicate worth a darn."

Autumn chuckled. "I'm guessing you were never the problem. Joy wants the finer things in life. Things a rancher can't provide." She pressed her lips together. "Trust me. Dallas is full of women like that." She rolled her eyes as though she'd seen as much during her recent stay in the big city.

Had the truths he'd been living by been false? Could Joy's words that had taken up residence in his mind be untrue?

"I guess Joy is part of the reason I'm frightened by what's happening with Laney."

Autumn offered a sad nod. "You were ready for marriage and kids. Joy was not. What's it going to take to get that through your thick noggin?" She waltzed away, taking some of Ethan's worry with her.

As he helped Earl with a few loads of iron partitions, he couldn't help but think, was Autumn right? Had his relationship with Joy been doomed from the start? Would a future with Laney be bright?

When they completed stacking the iron pieces, Ethan walked over to the drink tent for a break. Sweating and praying had brought a peace to Ethan about putting the past behind him and pursuing a future with Laney.

As he gulped down a sports drink, Laney approached. His heart did a little flip-flop. These days he felt like a teenage boy, all turned inside out by a girl.

A wide smile was on her face, showing a contentment that was the opposite of his ambitious ex-wife's. Laney seemed to fit right into small-town life. Though she was a city girl, Laney didn't look down her nose at the hardworking residents of Serenity like Joy had.

He had to stop comparing the two of them. They were nothing alike.

Truth was, a part of him was afraid of getting hurt again. But he refused to live in fear anymore.

Laney strolled over, beaming. The gentle breeze moved the light wisps of hair not pulled back into her loose ponytail. "I cannot believe you did this for me." She leaned in and softly kissed his cheek. Her smooth fingers touched his palm. Even though he longed to hold her hand again, he restrained himself. After what Autumn had said, he didn't want people gossiping about him and Laney.

His chest jackhammered. Whatever made him think he could dictate this thing between them? Or his feelings for her? They had definite chemistry and, frankly, that scared him.

"This is what Serenity does best. We come together." His voice didn't sound as airy and confident as he'd hoped—it was huskier and more unsure. Right then he realized their connection was like a sports car with no speed limit in sight, careening out of control.

A couple of hours ago, Laney had acknowledged an *us*. Then he had given her a sort of promise of a future kiss sometime soon. The whole thing excited him.

Esther, Earl's wife, stopped in front of them. "You two look cute together." She winked and moved on, leaving her words in her wake.

"See those clouds?" Laney pointed to the sky. "You don't think it'll rain, do you?"

White puffy clouds moved past as darker ones moved in. His stomach clenched. "Hope not."

"Hey, Ethan, I think we'll have time for that thing we talked about." Steve gave him a knowing glance.

"You're gonna like this." Ethan tilted his head toward the pavilion, again noticing the darkening sky. As they stepped around Theo and Earl, who worked at the circular saw cutting boards to replace rotted ones on the barn exterior, he pushed away the fear of the menacing clouds.

The gravel crunched under his boots, his heart rate pulsing in rhythm to his steps. Each time Laney's hand touched his, a flicker of attraction hit his senses. He could get used to this.

He and Laney rounded the corner of the barn and stepped toward the concrete pad Steve had poured last week, a beefy wood pillar embedded in each corner.

Laney sucked in an excited breath. "What? We're building the pavilion today, too?" She grabbed his hand and squeezed so hard it almost hurt.

"Yup. This is from the delivery a couple of days ago."

She smacked his arm. "I can't believe you kept this from me." Her gaze roamed around the area, taking in the four pillars coming out of the concrete. She could probably envision the completed structure she'd been dreaming about.

It might have taken losing Alice and Arthur to get where she was today, but Laney had a plan.

He no longer cared if the town gossiped. He grabbed her hand and brought it to his mouth, pressing a soft kiss on her knuckles. He delighted at her shy smile.

Pleasure at being a part of this event filled his core. Could he and Laney truly have a future together?

Gratefulness clung to Laney as she wandered the job site. All these people had come today to help her. They probably had chores at their own homes to do, but they had chosen to support her today. She'd be forever indebted to Serenity for their kindness.

"Barn is done," Steve yelled.

Hoots and hollers erupted from everyone on the property, especially the men collapsing the tall ladders they'd used to paint the top.

Laney took in the finished barn, looking stately covered in that red paint. She'd had no idea how much the supplies for a simple paint job could be, but it was worth every penny. "It's beautiful," she whispered.

Ethan squeezed her hand. "The day is going exactly as I planned it."

A breeze blew across her face, causing her to

gaze up again. The sudden gloominess of the day worried her. The sky seemed even darker now. *Please don't rain.*

The whir of drills, the whack of hammers and the sweet sound of townspeople chatting as they worked on various projects lifted from the property. *Her* property. Her heart was full. Maybe she had missed the blessing of being part of Serenity in the past, but she was thankful to be here now.

A deep rumble was heard in the distance. Unease churned in her stomach at the possibility of a storm. The day had been going so well.

Ethan caught her gaze, lines puckered between his eyes. "Was that—"

Thunder boomed.

Her chest tightened at the thought of everyone leaving.

"Everybody inside," Steve yelled.

People abandoned their posts and ran for cover.

"Oh, no," Laney whispered.

All the workers rushed to the porch, grabbing power tools as they ran. She forced her feet to move toward the safety of the covered porch as well.

"At least they finished painting the barn." Ethan's face looked pained at the turn of events.

Fat raindrops began to fall. Soon rain fell in sheets, and she could barely hear herself think.

But then Laney caught sight of the barn. She gasped.

The sides of the barn were now streaky with rain. Pools of red paint sat at the base of the building. "It's ruined," she croaked, though no one could make out her words over the din of the deluge.

"I guess the paint hadn't completely dried." She could barely hear Ethan's emotion-choked voice over the pounding rain.

Some volunteers jostled to get around them and into the house, where food waited.

As her pulse pounded in her ears, she clung to the wood railing. All that expensive paint, literally down the drain. Not only would she have to purchase the supplies again, but who knew when she'd get the volunteers or the super-tall ladders it took to cover the barn again? A tear traveled down her cheek, followed by another and another.

Knocking that task off her list would have been a huge accomplishment. Now she had no idea when it could happen again.

"What are we going to do?" she cried. "All this effort for nothing."

Ethan put his arm around her and squeezed. "Somehow we'll work it out."

She leaned her head against his strong shoulder, relieved she was able to share this burden.

Someone yelled for Ethan, and he moved into the house. As soon as he stepped away from her, she missed his touch. Missed his strength. Missed him.

What was she thinking?

She could not get involved with him.

Her goal was to concentrate on creating this wedding venue—she couldn't get derailed and lose the future she'd so carefully planned.

Somehow, she had to put a stop to whatever was happening between them.

Her gut burned at the washed-away paint, the loss of manpower and the damaged building supplies they hadn't had time to cover before this torrential downpour.

She had thought this workday would get them back on schedule, but boy, was she wrong.

The workday—and her personal life—had turned into a complete disaster.

Chapter Eleven

Ethan stifled a yawn at the exertion from corralling toddlers all day during the Fourth of July parade. Even though it hadn't required manual labor, like the workday at Laney's a week ago, his steps were dragging. He crouched down amid the candy wrappers littering the sidewalks to hug Tori and Zoe. The twins then reached for Laney, who stood beside him. "Be good for Memaw and Pops, okay?"

"We will, Daddy." They turned, hands clasped with their grandparents', and strolled to the truck. American flags hung from the old-timey light poles in town and crowds were dispersing in all different directions.

Relief poured from Ethan as he waved to the twins and his parents. "What a day. I adore my girls, but some days they can be exhausting."

He turned to Laney. "I couldn't have done it without you. Thank you for being here with me during the parade, to keep an eye on them. It takes a village." He laughed.

To get out of a family's way, he stepped closer to her, and his fingers brushed Laney's. His pulse galloped at the touch.

They'd reconnected over a month ago, but it felt like she'd always been here for him and the girls. And since the modern-day barn raising a week ago, something had clicked and moved their relationship forward. They had one more week of exchanging babysitting for work on the house. Then what?

"If I hadn't been here, people in town would have pitched in. No one would have allowed Tori or Zoe to get lost. I mean, how can you get lost here?" She twirled around on the sidewalk, seeming so happy.

"I think I'm more exhausted right now than after working a long day on the ranch." He rubbed a hand down his face, wishing for a nap after a hot day in the sun, yet he was unwilling to leave Laney for anything.

"Should we go home?" Her eyes rounded with concern.

He chuckled. "No. I'm looking forward to a meal without toddlers interrupting and an evening watching the town fireworks." He took her hand in his. "With you."

Somewhere along the way, he'd come to rely on her. Now he couldn't imagine life without her.

He felt like they were two magnets, unable to look away. The warmth from her smile drew him in. Was it because she cared, or was she simply kind to everyone?

"Maybe we should get something to eat from the food trucks?" She pointed across the way.

"Nope. Not tonight." He tugged her along with him. "Franco has a table saved for us."

There was a look of adoration on her face. "That's so sweet of you. I haven't been back to Eatalian Pizza since high school."

"Well, we're having a grown-up, sit-down meal. No food will be thrown on the floor, and no bibs or sippy cups will be involved. We might even have appetizers." He wiggled his brows at her.

She slapped his bicep. "You're trying to fatten me up."

"After all the running around after toddlers today, we deserve a five-course meal."

They strolled down the block in comfortable silence. Having her next to him felt so right. He had spoken with his mother about what Autumn said the other day about Joy. His mother appeared frustrated that he hadn't seen Joy for what she was.

"I can't thank you enough for the workday you organized last weekend. We got so much done. I mean, I have to purchase the paint and supplies for the barn again." She placed her hand over her heart. "But overall, it was a roaring success. And the free labor saved a ton of money, thanks to you."

He shrugged. "Seemed like the perfect thing to do, especially after the extra costs of the septic field and tank expansion."

"I couldn't believe everyone stayed until the rain ended and righted the supplies the storm ravaged. Then they somehow finished the pavilion. That was the icing on the cake."

"That's Serenity for you." Looking down the street, he flinched as he spotted his birth mother and maternal aunt. "There's Betty."

Laney sucked in a breath. "Where?" She scanned the crowd.

He indicated with his chin to a group in the distance.

"Do you ever see her?" she asked, gazing up at him.

"Nope. She never comes to family gatherings."

She widened her ocean-blue eyes. "I can't fathom that."

"Yup." Betty disappeared from the crowd, likely on her way home, like many people.

"How do you feel about her?"

He turned the question over in his head. "You know, the animosity I felt about her is slowly fading." He touched Laney's elbow and led her toward the restaurant. "I mean, she wasn't ready to be a parent then—still isn't. But I'm grateful for her decision to give me away so I'd have a better childhood."

Laney looked pensive. "So, do you feel like a real McCaw yet?" She rushed on. "I mean, I can't believe you ever felt that way." Her cheeks pinkened.

His little sister's friend had turned into an intelligent woman. A slow smile spread across his face, and his chest lightened. "Somehow in the past month, God showed me that my identity is in Christ." He wrinkled his nose. "When that happened, the importance of being a blood McCaw no longer mattered."

He *was* a real McCaw, in every way that counted. His parents loved him and his siblings equally. And they showed all their children that every day. Ethan needed to put his concern about not being a suitable son in the past, where it belonged.

They arrived at Eatalian Pizza.

"Enough of that." Ethan opened the door for Laney.

Patrons filled the space. Franco came over, the end of his skinny black tie shoved between two buttons. His stained white shirt had probably been spotless and starched at the beginning of the day.

He kissed them both on each cheek and enthused, *"È bello vederti."*

Ethan had been here enough times to know that the words meant *good to see you.* The scents of sauce, bread and Italian spices filled the air.

"I have a table for you. The booth in that back corner. See?" As soon as Ethan nodded and thanked him, Franco bustled off to help someone else.

They slid onto the curved vinyl bench, landing right next to each other. They studied their menus.

Ethan thought about each time he'd prayed for clarity about his now-defunct marriage. He felt like an eye doctor was changing his prescription so that he could see more clearly. He wasn't ready to agree Joy had been the problem, but he now believed he wasn't the only one at fault. God was pressing on him that taking the opinion of one selfish woman wasn't a wise way to live his life.

"Calamari. Yum," Laney stated as she put down her glossy menu in the center of the table next to his.

"The appetizer has been decided." He drank in the excited features on her face. Even after a grueling day chasing after the twins, she still had so much energy. He felt closer to wanting a relationship with Laney. When they were together, their connection felt organic and right.

No one had ever looked at him, including his ex-wife, with such love and respect. He hadn't realized how much he longed for that.

The waitress came and filled their water glasses. By the time they'd ordered—calamari and Caesar salad to share, pasta primavera for her and lasagna for him—the waitress had to fill up their water again. "Seems like everyone's thirsty today from being outside at the sun-filled parade. Did you all have fun?" She collected the menus.

Laney's and Ethan's gazes collided. Then they both chuckled.

"It was amazing," Ethan stated. "But with twin three-year-olds, we're pretty beat."

The teenage waitress cocked her head. "Oh, so date night. I'll get your food out fast so you can get a good seat for the town fireworks show."

Before Ethan could correct her assumption—
that he and Laney were married with twins—
she left.

In the background, music played, and people
talked and laughed. But he only had eyes for
Laney. "I'm glad you came back to Serenity."
He bumped her shoulder. Her hair tickled his
face as he was warmed with the thought of a
possible *them*. Should he push the feelings away
or embrace them?

"So am I. I had forgotten how close-knit
this community is. How everyone truly cares
about others." She straightened the silverware
in front of her. "I've also been enjoying my
time going to church and the women's midweek Bible study."

Franco returned. "Laney, I forgot to mention I changed the anniversary party menu just
a little. After I talked with Mabel, I realized
we were going to have too many starches on
the serving line. And you know how people
feel about carbohydrates these days." He patted
his belly. "So I switched out one of the pasta
dishes for chicken marsala. Cost won't change
by much. Is that okay with you?"

Laney's fingers flew to her lips. "Oh, Franco,
that sounds simply perfect." She rose and
hugged the jolly man.

Waitstaff yelled his name from across the room. "Gotta go." Franco took off faster than Ethan thought he could move.

Laney's eyes misted as she resettled next to him. "I cannot believe how kind people are being about this party. I mean, it's one thing to provide pasta at cost for the entire town, but chicken? That's so generous."

"Everyone loves Wade and Cora."

"No, it isn't just about them. It's this town. And how giving and caring it is."

He reached for Laney's hand. Their fingers laced together.

"How's camp? Only one week left."

Which meant only one more week of her nannying and him helping with construction. "Good. My mom's exhausted, but a good kind of exhausted, you know? So many people are helping her out. And my dad's on the mend."

He leaned forward and took in her gorgeous blue eyes that sucked him in as though they were the only two people in the room. He detected a faint whiff of her tantalizing perfume.

Yes, he liked Laney's company. He hadn't ever had a woman beam at him like she did. And he hungered for that.

"Serenity is amazing." She shook her head. "Everyone has welcomed me with open arms.

I have more people that I can turn to for help here than I ever had in San Antonio."

"Then I'm glad you've chosen to call Serenity your home." He rubbed his calloused thumb across the back of her smooth hand. He could get used to this real easy.

Seeing her compassionate reaction about the town made him more eager to pursue this relationship with Laney. He wanted to find out where it would lead.

Yes, he was still afraid of getting hurt, but based on what he had learned about Joy recently, he felt more confident about giving love another shot.

Stuffed, Laney made her way through the Italian restaurant. What an amazing meal. She would have taken home leftovers, but they'd be at the football field to watch fireworks before she returned home.

Ethan opened the door for Laney. Then he placed his hand on the small of her back as they walked out the door.

She was thrilled by it. Was this what having a healthy relationship with a man felt like? To lean on someone who respected you as much as you respected him?

Her mind returned to the conversation she'd

had with Cora midweek. Laney had expressed her concerns about getting involved with Ethan. Her fear that she'd get derailed from her work at the wedding venue. That she'd put her needs above God's and, in the process, lose herself.

Cora's wisdom prevailed. The older woman had reminded Laney to set her sights on God, not on an earthly relationship.

She nodded, full of peace and ready for whatever may come.

"It sure was nice of Alyssa to give us these." She lifted her foam cup full of ice water to bring along to the fireworks. Fresh air replaced the Italian food smells from the restaurant.

"She's a great waitress."

"Is she one of Franco's daughters?" she asked as she paused at the bottom of the steps for Ethan.

"The oldest." He turned left toward the high school. She followed.

As they walked, he reached out and caught her hand in his. His skin was rough and calloused, exactly what she expected a cowboy's hand to feel like.

"Is the construction project still in the red?"

"Yes, spiraling out of control as we speak." She chuckled. "But if it weren't for the workday, thank you again for that, I'd be even more off budget."

"Well, you're handling it pretty well."

"Thanks to you." What would she do without Ethan? All his construction help. And planning the workday. She was forever indebted to him.

"Now that you've been here a month, do you miss your life in San Antonio?" he queried.

"Some parts."

"I don't feel like I know much about your past."

On their free evenings, they had already talked about how she had loved her event-planning job but had become a workaholic and how her friend Rose had grounded her. But she hadn't shared about her prior romantic failure. "I dated a man who misused my trust." Similar to Joy.

He stopped. "You can tell me if you want, you know."

Though the concern over where their relationship might lead—if anywhere—was real, the gentleness in his tone turned her to mush. She had to move on sometime. Why not now? Why not with Ethan?

"Turned out he was married with kids. And I never had a clue. He was good at lying to me."

"He sounds like a jerk. And I'm so sorry. Not all men are like that." He rubbed her thumb. The sweet touch wound through her.

She was grateful Ethan cared. Grateful she'd come back to Serenity. This past month, back in her childhood happy place, had not only been a walk down memory lane, but an opportunity for her to see what home really stood for. Peace and contentment. Family and love. Cherishing others like they cherished you.

They passed Imagination Station. "Think you might get the twins the dollhouse they love so much?" When she pointed at the toy store window, she recalled the day the store clerk had thought they were a family. Glancing at their clasped hands gave Laney hope for the future.

He tossed his head back and laughed. "Nope. Now they want a play kitchen. Kind of like this one." He pointed at the display window, where a gorgeous wooden kitchen sat.

"I love that."

"Maybe for Christmas I'll get them one of those plastic kitchen sets." He shrugged.

She sighed. Being with this man brought her such joy. She thanked God for bringing him into her life.

As they approached the high school, he squeezed her hand. "I'm glad Autumn is saving us space on the family blanket. Looks like a big turnout." He flashed an easy smile at her as though her poor past decisions didn't faze him.

They walked single file around a group of people chatting, staying with the crowd heading to the high school football field to watch the fireworks. A year ago, Laney had watched the televised Independence Day fireworks from the nation's capital. Alone. With a bowl of popcorn.

To be here tonight, in this town that felt more and more like home every day, touched her deeply. Had her aunt and uncle not passed away, would she still be living in San Antonio?

The sermon on Sunday had been about how Joseph's brothers sold him for twenty shekels. What they meant for harm, God turned into good. It made Laney consider the many things she thought of as bad: Aunt Alice's and Uncle Arthur's deaths, choosing to stay in San Antonio to work and her relationship with her ex-boyfriend. But she could see the good that had come about from all three. In many ways.

"Laney," a voice called from behind.

She turned and spotted Opal, the gray-haired receptionist from First Church. She dropped Ethan's hand and hugged Opal in greeting.

"I've heard a large buzz from the community about Cora and Wade's party."

"Oh, no. I hope someone doesn't spoil the surprise." They'd all worked so hard to plan this event. It'd be a shame if the honorees learned about it before the surprise party.

Opal shook her head. "Nothing like that. I meant to say, it sounds like the turnout is going to be bigger than we predicted. Are you okay if we set up more tables and chairs?"

"Of course, Opal. It's heartwarming to see everyone come together for their anniversary like this." Unshed tears swam in her eyes, and she willed them to evaporate. No one needed to know how desperately she was falling in love with this town.

"Then it's a plan. Do you need to update the drawing you gave me?" At Laney's shake of the head, she continued. "Okay, I'll let you two skedaddle. Moe said Autumn is at the football field saving your seats, so I guess you don't need to hurry." The older woman scurried away.

"How does her husband know…?"

Ethan bumped her shoulder. "That's part of small towns. Everyone knows everyone's business." He winked.

The wink made her smile. Was he feeling the same attraction as she was?

The jingle of an ice cream truck sounded, followed by children's giggles. They squeezed past the kids, waiting in line for their frozen treats. "Zoe and Tori would love this."

"Sometimes when we're in town, Ray is here, so they've experienced it."

Her thoughts wandered back to Opal. To the time they'd spent together organizing the number of chairs and tables needed. Finally, she had found a wise person who wasn't a McCaw, so she'd asked Opal to counsel her on renewing the lease agreement. They discussed Laney's concern over lack of control and she was close to telling Ethan the land was all his.

Ethan placed his palm on her back to lead her around another group of people standing and talking. Such a gentleman. He'd never turn into someone like her ex-boyfriend.

"I found a box of framed photos in the guest room clutter." She would not cry. "Some were posed pictures of Aunt Alice and Uncle Arthur. But many of them were candid shots of them taking part in town events. Did you know Arthur won her basket at the picnic lunch silent auction when they were seniors in high school?"

His earnest face was so sweet, it wrapped her in an invisible warmth. "I do. They loved to tell that story."

"I believe that was the earliest photo of them as a couple." Laney cherished the fond memories of her aunt and uncle.

"My mother laments the digital age, because

people don't get physical photographs as much anymore."

She never had a photo album growing up. As an adult, she never had pictures to put in it. So few friends. So few memory-making moments. "That's probably why I've thoroughly enjoyed going through my aunt's photo albums. And framed candid photos."

Now at the football field, she dodged a group of rowdy high schoolers, Ethan right behind. She glanced at him. "They really loved this town."

"They did." His eyes crinkled. "There's Autumn." Ethan tugged her to the center of the field.

She and Autumn hugged hello. Something about her relationship with Ethan's sister felt like forever, kind of how she was starting to think her feelings for Ethan were.

They settled on the blanket, and Ethan draped his arm around her shoulders. What would it be like to be a part of the McCaw family—and mother to Zoe and Tori?

She couldn't say for sure, but the idea had taken hold in her heart.

What if she let her guard down and saw what happened with Ethan? Perhaps the future would surprise her.

Chapter Twelve

Ethan's heart raced at his concern over Laney. Fat raindrops splattered his windshield. He flipped the wipers to the highest speed. When Laney was a no-show at the big house for Monday night family dinner, he hadn't worried too much. But he became more anxious that something might have happened on her ranch when he texted her and didn't get a reply. He turned into her lane.

His mother's beef Stroganoff churned in his stomach. Either heartburn or he was unsettled over Laney's safety. He stopped beside her empty sedan and rushed to the house, dodging the rain. The porch sat empty and uninviting.

He rapped on the door and then let himself in. "Laney! Are you okay?" He barged through the shadowy kitchen, the air-conditioning chilling his damp skin. He tossed his hat onto the laminate counter.

In the living room, he spotted Laney weeping. A standing lamp in the far corner lit the space that had been darkened by the evening storm. He rushed over to her. "Honey, are you hurt? What's wrong?"

"I'm fine." Her voice broke as she threw her arms around him. "I should have come back to visit more often," she mumbled through his shirt.

He drew in a tight, audible breath. So much for guarding his heart. "Now stop. Alice and Arthur loved you," he whispered.

Of course, he wanted her to stop crying, to not feel so wounded, but holding her in his arms felt so right.

"I know that. I do." She hiccuped a couple of breaths and then sank deeper against him. "But I missed out on so much by working seven days a week."

"Well, you couldn't help it. The job owned you." Her head fit under his chin perfectly. He made small soothing circles on her back, like he did to the twins. Except this situation felt completely different. This was a woman he thought he loved. He put his thoughts aside to give her his full attention.

"Ranching is the same. You can't call your

hours when you work with animals." As her sobbing grew harder, his insides ripped apart at her heartbreaking tears.

Her messy ponytail bobbed with each breath she took. The wildflower perfume that had scared him a month ago now drew him in. As each day passed, he realized he wanted to be near this tantalizing smell forever.

"But that's just it. I allowed my manager to abuse my time. I always made myself available and did special projects because I wanted to be noticed. To be promoted." She leaned back, her gaze dropping to a photo album on her lap. "See all the events in their lives that I missed?"

Birthdays. Anniversaries. Town events. Everyday life.

"They knew how much you loved them." He wondered where this was all coming from. Hadn't she gone through this stage of grief weeks ago?

"But I missed so much. And now they're gone." Her lower lip trembled. Then she glanced at him.

He reached out and held her hand.

Though the room was still a construction zone, a spider plant hung in the corner, and another wide, leafy green plant sat on the repainted fireplace hearth. Slowly, Laney was making the space cozy.

She jumped up. "I need to get out of here." She took off, leaving her girlie scent in her wake.

For a city gal, she seemed to enjoy fresh air and wide-open spaces. He grabbed his Stetson, followed her out the door and settled on the swing while she paced the length of the porch. The rain had slowed to a sprinkle.

She stopped in front of him and wrinkled her nose. "Rose got engaged last night."

"Your friend from San Antonio? The finance lady?"

She nodded, her face colored with confusion. "She wants to have her wedding here. It lines up with when I was thinking of opening the venue."

"That's a good thing. What better grand opening than your best friend's wedding?" He wasn't sure what was happening here. All the tears and her sad face. He balanced his hat on his right knee.

"Aunt Alice won't be here," she said, worrying her hands.

Ah, that was it. She had waited too long, and Alice wouldn't be here to share in the grand opening.

"If only I had come back a year or two ago." She looked unsure.

"You may not have come back, but I'm sure Alice enjoyed talking with you about the renovation for years. Seems like that brought her great joy."

"We did talk pretty frequently about the venue."

"You know the Scripture verse that states God has a plan for each of us? How He plans to give us a future and a hope?" She nodded. "God knew when you'd be ready to move here."

"But what if I haven't been following God's leading? What if His plan had me coming back five years ago?" Her chin wobbled.

"Maybe. But maybe He gave you this ranch and a project to work on while you grieved two people you loved dearly." He cradled her hands in his. "Maybe this is *all* God's timing." Including a relationship between the two of them.

Her forehead wrinkles vanished as she wiped the last of her tears away. "Maybe you're right." She cocked her head to the side. "Aunt Alice and I relished envisioning this new business."

He grinned at her light-bulb moment.

"Doing all this with my aunt and uncle here would have disrupted their retirement." She plopped down beside him.

"So true." That she would share this revelation with him sparked a rush of adrenaline.

She leaned her head against his shoulder.

Her nearness made his senses spin. The breadth of how Laney cherished people drew him closer. He shifted and put his arm around her, tugging her close.

"Thank you. Thank you for checking on me tonight and for helping me figure things out."

His heart hammered in his chest. He gazed into her eyes and realized he had fallen in love with Laney. A calm descended on him. This felt like the real deal. "My pleasure."

He knew what he wanted—a future with Laney. And he'd do everything in his power to make that happen.

God had given him a second chance at love, and he would accept it with open arms.

When Ace began barking, Laney jumped to her feet.

"What is it, Ace?" She looked in the direction the dog faced as Ethan's footsteps tapped behind her. With cloudy skies and a steady rain, all she could see were fields. The ones Ethan leased were a lush green.

"You silly goose," she said to the dog. "I don't see a thing." The smell of Ethan's spicy cologne drifted over. He'd probably cleaned up and shaved before dinner, because his face was clear of stubble.

She stepped off the porch and pulled the elastic out of her hair, letting it fall over her shoulders in natural waves. Though she was thankful Ethan had come looking for her, the butterflies that took flight in her belly scared her. How could she have begun to care for him so much in such a short time? "Come here, boy," she called to Ace.

Ace turned and ran to her. Ever since she'd heard about the copperhead, she'd tried to keep the dog closer to the house. She had purchased a cooling bed and laid it on the covered porch. The dog spent most of his days lazing on his new nest.

Her stomach rumbled. She had missed dinner. Again. But it didn't matter, because she finally felt at peace about not starting the wedding venue earlier. "Thanks for helping me realize the timing of the renovation was probably a God thing."

"Happy to." Ethan sported a blue-and-green-checked chambray shirt, sleeves rolled up to his elbows, with jeans, cowboy boots and his ever-present wide leather belt with a silver buckle. His satisfied grin warmed her core.

She ruffled Ace's fur as they retreated to the cover of the porch. "It's still pretty hot today."

"That's July in Texas. The cooler weather we had after sunset these past few weeks won't happen again until the end of August, maybe even September." He settled on the swing, leaving space for her. Except she wasn't ready to join him. Not yet.

Ace circled in his bed three times before lying down.

Laney rested against a column. "Sorry about all that crying in there." She nodded to the door and the embarrassing display from earlier. She longed to sit beside him and have him comfort her worries away like he had inside, but unease kept her planted in place, her bare feet warm against the damp porch floorboards.

"No problem. Alice and Arthur were good people. I miss them, too."

"You know, this place was my refuge." A lump formed in her throat at the thought of the very first time she'd visited. Her aunt had decorated a room in pink for Laney. Children's books filled the bookcase, plush stuffed animals decorated the bed and the softest beanbag chair occupied one corner. She had spent hours by herself reading. The one skill she possessed as a child was being able to read and tune out the world. Then she grew older and attended Cora's Victory Youth Camp, made friends and saved reading for the torturous months of the year back home. "I can't tell you how much this ranch, Cora's camp and you McCaws changed my life." They'd given her hope when her life had been so very dark.

Ethan leaned forward, elbows on knees. "You were part of the family." The sparkle in his eyes proved his sincerity.

She'd be forever grateful for the McCaws.

Laney had always thought she was a city girl. It was one of the things that had held her back from coming here to start her venue. And boy, was she wrong. As it turned out, she was a country girl all the way.

"This past month has reminded me how much Serenity means to me." Laney's throat constricted. She didn't feel worthy to be a part of this community.

"It's nice out here. Without the girls. Alone with you." He straightened, his arm draped along the back of the swing, as if inviting her over. His ever-present Stetson was perched on his right knee.

Suddenly she needed to tell him about her decision. She wanted nothing unsaid between them. "Since the lease money will pay for the property tax and upkeep, I'm going to renew your land lease."

The light in his eyes had dimmed. Maybe he had expected her to say something about her feelings.

"I decided to just use that one ceremony spot, with the more narrow walking path to it. You'll have to move your fences, but I think we can both share the land."

"Thank you, Laney. My family thanks you, too." He scrubbed his face.

A breeze blew, lifting her hair. She smoothed it down as she strode over and sat on the swing. The part she was afraid to say out loud was that she wanted to see where their relationship was headed. Because she thought she was falling in love.

He slipped his arm around her shoulders and gazed into her eyes. Then he lowered his head and pressed his lips to hers.

The sensation reminded her of the fireworks the other night. But better. The trepidation she had about her romantic feelings fell away.

When he pulled back, she could see emotions shining in his eyes. So this was love.

A calm threaded through her, along with hope for the future. She had never felt calm about prior relationships—she'd always been unsure. She'd always thought vulnerability exposed your weaknesses. Now she knew it took a lot more courage to allow someone into your heart. Was she ready for this?

Laney knew, deep in her soul, that she was home. Ethan and the twins and Serenity were her future.

She heard a throat clearing and jumped away. Autumn climbed the steps with a devilish grin on her face.

"Maybe it's a good thing I was working and couldn't get here until now?" She smirked.

In the depths of her grief, Laney had texted Autumn, asking her to come over. She couldn't take being alone with her thoughts and memories a moment longer. Shortly after sending the text, Ethan had arrived.

"Looks like my big brother helped out better than I could have done." She wiggled her eyebrows.

Laney's cheeks heated as she stood. "It's not what you think."

Except it was exactly what Autumn was thinking. She'd fallen in love with Ethan. And there was no going back.

Chapter Thirteen

As Laney loaded the twins into the double stroller, anticipation hummed in her chest at seeing Ethan. Their kiss the other day replayed in her mind. And she wanted more of that same thing.

"Laney," a voice called out.

She turned to find Autumn walking toward her. The girls clapped at her and chanted, "Tum, Tum."

"Love the pint-size cowboy boots. Pink and purple. So apropos." Autumn gave each toddler a kiss on the cheek. "Where are you all off to?"

"I thought it'd be nice to take the girls on a little impromptu picnic." She felt heat rise in her cheeks. Should she mention they were going to surprise Ethan? No. She didn't want her friend reading into it too much.

"We go see Daddy," Zoe supplied as she pointed her electric-pink cowboy boots toward the barn.

Autumn gave her a knowing smile. The tips of Laney's ears burned.

What did Autumn think—that they'd kiss in front of the girls? She slid the cooler under the stroller as the kids kicked their little boots, impatient to get going. After she dropped her water bottle into the holder and released the locked wheel, she grabbed the jogger handle. "We've got to get to the barn before Ethan leaves. I can see his location right now, but I don't know when he's leaving again."

Autumn jerked her head back. "He added you on his tracker?"

"Of course. I'm watching his kids."

She nodded.

Laney pushed the stroller forward and crossed the stepping-stones between the two homes. "See you later," she called to Autumn, ignoring her friend's penetrating gaze and pointed questions.

At the end of the properties, she turned left onto the gravel path.

"Goats?" Zoe said.

"Pwease?" came from Tori.

"On the way back." The goats bleated as

they passed. The miniature horses grunted and snorted to get their attention. "Give us thirty minutes and then we'll pet you. Maybe even some table scraps if you're good." She winked at Pinky Pie. She still couldn't believe Ethan had named the animal after his daughters' favorite stuffed unicorns. Yes, they both used the same name for their identical toys.

She held her breath as they passed the chicken coop.

"Chickens?" Zoe asked.

"Pwease?" Tori said once again.

"No, I'm sorry, girls, but we've talked about that aggressive rooster." She'd recommended gifting the rooster to a nearby rancher who didn't have children. "You need an adult." And not her. Even though Ethan said the rooster was only belligerent to youngsters, he'd chased Laney out of the coop.

"You! You!" Zoe stated.

"How about I ask Daddy to take you after your nap?"

"'Kay," the twins said in unison.

How could this be her last week to watch the girls? The last week to get sweet snuggles from them. Six weeks had flown by. She wasn't looking forward to Friday afternoon, the end of her nannying gig. What would she do without Zoe and Tori? Without seeing Ethan every morning and working alongside him every afternoon? But a deal was a deal. Friday ended their arrangement.

Laney turned right, onto the pavement, and headed up to the barn.

The girls started calling for their father. So much for the surprise.

At the entrance, Ethan shaded his eyes, a bridle and cloth in his hands. He caught her gaze and grinned. "Lookie here, it's my favorite girls." He winked at her and then the twins.

Her heart drummed against her rib cage at his attention. "We brought lunch." She locked the stroller wheels.

"Picnic," the girls stated in unison. They started wiggling to get out of their stroller.

"A picnic, huh?" He helped her with the straps, and they freed the twins, who began chasing each other in circles.

Ethan helped Laney with the quilt, cooler and basket. They found a flat area for the quilt and anchored it with the cooler and basket. His dancing eyes spoke of his delight at their visit.

Every day since the kiss, their relationship had progressed by baby steps, which was fine with her, because she was in no hurry. She was excited about the future with him and the twins.

The girls rushed over, and Ethan lifted each with one arm.

"Can we have cawots?" Zoe asked.

"To feed the hawses?" Tori added.

Ethan handed them fresh carrots.

The girls walked into the barn, their brightly colored cowboy boots slipping with each step they took. Once in the barn, they giggled and jumped back as each horse most likely tickled their hand while taking the offered carrot.

"They are so adorable."

"I agree. Though I'm a little partial." He caught her hand and squeezed. "Thanks for thinking of this. I appreciate it."

His touch sent a warming shiver through her.

The respect and tenderness in his eyes just about did her in. Was this true love? Could she let her defenses down and trust Ethan with her heart?

"My pleasure." She loved spending time with him. Whether it be caring for the girls, eating at the big house, taking a walk or sitting on the porch swing talking.

He pushed an errant lock of hair behind her ear. Her breath stalled in her lungs.

"It's amazing we've only known each other a little over a month. I mean, since you've returned to town."

His words broke the moment and reminded her of what Autumn had said about Joy the other day at a garage sale. She slipped on her sunglasses and settled on the quilt. "I've been wondering, how long did you know Joy before you got married?"

He rubbed the back of his neck and sat, eyeing the entrance to the barn where the girls were located. "We knew each other for a few years, but she wasn't on my radar at first." His face clouded. "Once I noticed her, things moved pretty quick."

"What do you mean, she wasn't on your radar?" Laney lifted the basket and pulled out the plastic plates.

He shrugged. "I don't know, but at a horse show, her sister took me aside and mentioned Joy liked me." He fingered the several days' growth of beard on his chin, drawing her attention to the growing stubble.

"So that was the start?" Something about this story concerned her. Something seemed off.

"Yup. My family tried to warn me about Joy, especially Autumn."

"But you didn't listen."

"No. Joy said all the right things. Looking back, I have to admit we barely knew each other on the day of our wedding."

Laney sucked in a breath. "How is that possible?"

"We got engaged two weeks after her sister approached me."

"Why?"

He shifted, as though uncomfortable. "Because she asked me to marry her. I agreed, and then she came up with a story about how I was the one who proposed. That was the tale we told everyone. I confided the truth in my mother, but it was too late at that point."

"Two weeks?"

"Yup. We got married a month later. She thought it'd be fun to get married on the one-month anniversary of our engagement."

How in the world had Ethan married someone so fast? It had taken him over a month to kiss Laney.

Unease crawled up her spine. Maybe giving her whole heart to him was not a good idea.

"She spent our engagement planning this big wedding. The fanciest shindig I've ever been to." He gazed into the pasture. "I was in charge of the honeymoon. We went to a bed-and-breakfast a couple of towns away, and that didn't go over well with her at all." He shook his head. "She had wanted to fly somewhere, apparently over a body of water, and stay in some fancy hotel."

"I can't see you in Paris or at a fancy Caribbean resort."

"Those were two of the places she mentioned." He chuckled. "She couldn't believe the Triple C owner didn't want to indulge a little."

Laney wondered if the reason Joy had wanted to marry Ethan was his ownership stake in the ranch. Maybe Joy actually thought the Triple C was a moneymaker? If so, she had been dead wrong. Maybe once she realized the McCaws weren't wealthy, she'd had no reason to stay?

Regardless, Ethan had made a reckless decision. "Seems you two were an odd match."

"She was gorgeous. I guess I never imagined someone like that would even consider me."

Her breath caught. "That's a shallow reason for making an important life decision."

He flinched. And then, when he called the girls to come eat, he scowled at her. Zoe raced to them, Tori lagging behind until he counted to three.

Laney put her head down and focused on serving up food and tried hard to ignore the warning signs flashing like a railroad crossing in front of her.

His quick rush into marriage with someone

who clearly wasn't right for him turned Laney's excitement into apprehension.

Because the last time engaging brown eyes and smoldering chemistry took over her life, things hadn't ended so well. She'd made a mistake trusting a man before, and she didn't want to repeat the same mistake again.

She couldn't trust her judgment. The past had proved that.

Right now, she wanted to run far away, but felt frozen in place.

Ethan watched as Laney pulled out cold fried chicken, macaroni and cheese, hush puppies and frosted brownies—all his favorite foods. He sniffed the tasty aroma as a heavy weight settled in his stomach. Her stinging comment—*that's a shallow reason for making an important life decision*—swirled in his brain.

What bothered him the most was that she was right. Dead right.

A vise tightened around his heart. He wasn't good at relationships. What was he doing carrying on with Laney like this?

"I'm thirsty," Zoe said.

Laney passed her a juice box.

And just like that, he realized he needed to ignore his emotions and enjoy the moment. His babies would only be three for a little while longer. He surveyed the quilt, the food and the thoughtfulness that went into this little feast. "Wow, this looks fabulous."

"Thank Mabel for the fried chicken and hush puppies. I won't ever try to make either item at home when she has perfected them." Laney whipped out baby wipes and cleaned Tori's and Zoe's hands before they started to eat.

"So not really impromptu, since Monday's special is fried chicken at Mabel's Diner and today is Wednesday?"

A flush crept up her adorable cheeks. "I kinda planned it. Called Mabel yesterday to place a special order."

"Either way, thank you. It makes it a bit more special to know that you were thinking of this yesterday." His hand covered hers. Was he being too bold, especially after her harsh words?

After flashing a worried glance at the twins, she whisked her hand away. "Girls, stay on the blanket while we eat. Zoe, you have the blue square, since you like the blueberry bars. Tori, scoot over to the red one, since you favor raspberry bars." Her commanding voice was reserved for the twins.

The girls studied the quilt below them and

centered themselves on their squares. He found it amazing he was learning parenting tricks from someone who wasn't yet a parent.

Her earlier question about Joy buzzed around in his head like a persistent horsefly. His chest still pounded at stating his failures out loud a few minutes ago. It forced him to question himself, and the idea of a relationship, all over again. Maybe instead of growing closer to Laney, he should back off.

She passed a plate filled with bite-size chunks of chicken, hush puppies and grapes cut in half to Tori, then a more organized one to Zoe, who didn't like her foods to touch. They both thanked her.

His twins had flourished under Laney's care these past six weeks. She'd taught his girls to write their letters, sing the alphabet song, pick up their toys before meals, and made obedience a fun game.

They all bowed while he said a quick blessing before they ate. A chorus of amens came from his three girls.

Laney handed him a plate piled high with food. "For the working cowboy who needs calories." She grinned. Seemed her earlier displeasure at his decisions surrounding Joy had landed on the back burner. He wished it would stay there.

"I can't believe I only have two days left with the girls."

"You can still see them—you just won't need to get up at the crack of dawn anymore."

"I'd like that." At that moment, she seemed almost shy.

"It's been fun working together, hasn't it?" He'd miss their time tackling items from her growing to-do list, their private talks and the hope of their hands brushing, which caused feelings he hadn't felt in years to rise. Would she choose to spend time with him once their arrangement was over?

"Thank you so much for helping me with the renovation. We have gotten so much more accomplished than I ever dreamed. And of course, the workday where you practically recruited the entire town." She laid her hand on top of his and interlaced their fingers. "It's nice to have friends."

So she considered him just a friend? Part of him was okay with that. The other part could not stop thinking about their kiss the other day. He rubbed his thumb against her skin.

She tossed him a demure look as she untangled her hand and fixed herself a plate of food. "I can't wait for the anniversary party on Saturday. It's been a much more relaxed event to plan. I'm not sure if it's the pace of this town or that so many are volunteers. But it has been a dream to organize."

"My mom is going to be thrilled. Dad will probably wish they stayed home and watched TV."

Within minutes, the twins declared themselves done eating and asked to be excused from the quilt. "Yes, girls," he said. "You did a great job. Stay out here where we can see you, okay?"

Noticing Laney had finished her food, he wolfed down the rest of his lunch, then helped her clean up.

"Girls, that's too far away," Laney called to them. "See that big rock? Yes, that's the one. Stay between me and the rock, okay?"

"You're so good with them. A natural."

She set the folded quilt under the stroller. "They're easy to love."

Suddenly, he could see the four of them as a family. A couple of days ago, the thought would have made him ecstatic, but today trepidation wound through his chest. Her questions about Joy pointed out that their relationship was moving much too fast. Things between him and Laney needed to slow down.

"The cooler goes right there." She pointed.

He slid the cooler next to the picnic basket.

"Thanks again. This was such a surprise. And so sweet." He wanted to hug her, but the ranch hands were roaming about too close.

"You're welcome." She raised her voice. "Girls, it's time to go." She touched his arm. "I told them you'd take them to the chicken coop after their nap."

"Sure, no problem." He leaned closer and got a whiff of her floral perfume. "Still afraid of that rooster?"

She swatted his arm. "He's scary. Admit it, Mr. Chicken Whisperer."

"That's Mr. Rooster Whisperer to you."

She laughed. Oh, he could get used to that sound.

The girls crashed into his legs. He squatted and squeezed each of them. "I'll be home in about an hour."

"Can we go to the—"

"Chicken coop after your nap? Yes, indeed."

He helped Laney buckle them in their seats. "You sure you have this? It has to be heavy with the cooler and all."

"It's a jogging stroller. It's meant for off-roading. We'll see you soon." Her casual grin held contentment.

He waved as they made the brief trip back to his house.

Yes, the picnic had been nice. Very nice. But talking about the demise of his marriage had reopened an old wound and reminded him of his flaws.

If he were to talk about this with his mother, she'd rightly state Joy had conned him. But Laney was authentic, the real thing.

The more time he spent with Laney, the deeper he fell in love. And that scared him to the core.

He shook his head, trying to rid himself of his powerful attraction to Laney, but it seemed here to stay.

What if he took a chance on love and got burned again? Could he survive that a second time?

Or should he embrace whatever was happening between them and enjoy the moment?

Chapter Fourteen

The sun sat low in the sky as the illuminated string lights began to shine. Country music could be heard playing from the gazebo. The anniversary party was underway.

"Laney did an amazing job organizing this event," Ethan said to his sister. "Even though the entire town is here, it still feels intimate."

"I can't believe we kept this a surprise from Mom and Dad." Autumn had a calm air about her tonight. "Did you see how happy they were?"

Ethan chuckled. "That was all you and Laney. Mostly Laney."

"So true. She is an event planner at heart. I mean, even if she hadn't chosen it for a living, she has a talent for organizing and party planning." Autumn grasped her long hair in her hands and twisted it in a knot on top of her head.

He could smell the enticing foods from the

buffet as he scanned the crowd, looking for Laney. She was across the square helping an older couple find some seats. The sundress she wore matched the color of her eyes, and her updo made her even more beautiful.

Laney had been so busy preparing for today and then directing things when the event started that he'd barely spoken to her. She appeared in her element, making sure everyone had everything they needed.

Finally, love no longer scared him. Excitement about the future hummed underneath his rib cage.

"You love her, don't you?" Autumn's soft voice interrupted his thoughts of Laney and how content she appeared at this small-town gathering.

The moment hung in the air as Autumn's head cocked to the side.

His eyes connected with Autumn's. "Maybe." He was afraid to agree. Afraid something was about to go horribly wrong.

"You two make a great team."

His thoughts flew to recent conversations with his sister and mother. About Joy. About how Ethan had been too hard on himself. His gaze flickered to Laney. "It saddens me that Joy and I were never a team. She was only looking out for herself."

Autumn gave him a side hug. "I hate that you went through all that. But if not for you and Joy, we wouldn't have Tori and Zoe."

"Amen." The past month had been a time of self-discovery for him. In fact, his mother thought it was because of Laney's arrival and their growing feelings for each other.

Autumn nodded and tossed him a contented smile. "I have a good feeling about the two of you."

"Don't get too ahead of yourself."

"I'm not." She set her worried gaze on him. "With Dad's concussion, you've had a stressful month."

His mother approached them, arm linked with Dad's. "He sure did."

"I'm all better now," his father stated. "Ready to get back on a horse. You wouldn't think a man would miss riding so much, but I sure did."

"I am thrilled you'll be back on Monday."

"Here you are, my favorite family." Laney joined the crowd. She sidled up to Ethan, and he clasped his hand with hers.

Her soft fingers rubbed against his weathered ones. He could smell the floral scent of her perfume. How had he gotten so blessed as to have her by his side?

"Laney, thank you so much for this wonderful party," Mom gushed.

"Were you surprised?"

"You betcha." Wade grinned.

"Oh, sweetie, it couldn't have been better." His mother hugged Laney.

A pride Ethan couldn't explain washed over him. She *had* done an amazing job from start to finish.

Opal came over and asked Laney for help, so she left. Then Mom and Dad went off to visit with more friends.

"I knew they were surprised," Autumn stated. "Oh, there's Walker. I need to ask him about the band." She walked away.

"Hey, Ethan, how's the bull doing today?" Their local veterinarian ambled up to him.

He swung his gaze over to Earl, who'd been at their ranch late into last night with a bull who had gotten tangled up with a barbed-wire fence. "Much better. Thank you for stitching him and the injectable antibiotics. He's acting like nothing ever happened."

Earl chuckled. "Good. That was the plan."

Across the square, the town playboy approached Laney. Conrad Vaughn. Did they know each other? Conrad had grown up here—he had a fancy getaway on the edge of town but lived most of the time in a swanky penthouse in Dallas. Apparently, he had founded a computer security firm. Ethan's baby brother, Walker, worked for Conrad and seemed to like the guy.

Since Conrad had made it big and still called Serenity his home—at least part-time—the town considered him their local hero.

"Did you try the tiramisu?" Earl patted his belly. "I was thinking of having seconds. Want some?"

Ethan shook his head, unable to take his eyes off Conrad. When he leaned in to say something to Laney, thoughts of Joy trying to get her claws into Conrad came to mind. Though Conrad would have none of it, that moment made Ethan realize his wife had wanted more than he could ever have provided.

He feared Laney would become bored with him and want to return to her city life.

Why was Laney even talking to Conrad? She handed her phone over to him and laughed. Ethan took a step back in surprise.

She was chatting with Conrad like he was an old friend. Their conversation reminded him of the ones Joy had when she flirted with the man right before she up and left, picking at Ethan's painful scabs from the past.

Ethan ground his back molars together. He

hadn't wanted to fall in love, and yet here he was, in love with a city gal. Would she always long for more, just like Joy? Would Laney grow tired of the simple life and want her city life back?

His thoughts flitted to the extra jobs Laney kept doing for San Antonio people.

He hoped Serenity would be enough for Laney, but he'd been wrong in the past.

Would she leave and break his heart?

"Yes, all of it," Laney said for probably the third time. Did Conrad not believe her? This event was just a simple little anniversary party. He made it sound like she'd arranged the queen's coronation or something.

The event had been easier to plan than Laney thought. She gazed around the space and enjoyed the gentle conversation of so many people who loved Cora and Wade as much as she did.

She tucked her phone away. This chitchat with Conrad Vaughn felt more like an interview than casual conversation. Maybe that was how the Texas tech guru acted, always in business mode? She wasn't sure, but she hadn't seen Ethan in a bit, and she wanted to find him.

She still felt bad about how quick she'd been to judge him the other day when they discussed his decisions around marrying Joy. Laney liked him. A lot. Maybe even loved him. And he didn't need her judging his past—he did that just fine on his own.

"So, Laney, here's the thing," Conrad's deep voice rumbled. "I've been looking for an event coordinator for a while now. And I think you're it."

"Me? I'm sorry, but I gave that up to start a wedding venue here in town."

"I understand. But my sources tell me you are only planning on Saturday weddings and, at most, two Sundays a month."

Her mouth dropped open. Not too many people knew about her specific plans.

"Listen, I need someone I can trust. This—" He spread his arms wide. "This is not my forte."

"Like I said, I'm starting a business here. In Serenity."

"I respect that. And I'm not asking you to work for me forever. Just a year, until you bring on a staff and hire someone trustworthy to replace you."

She was shocked at his generous offer. "You own a security company. What do you need with a staff of event planners?"

"Security positions have become competitive. Yes, I can offer higher salaries, but to entice the best of the best, I also provide workers with a remote option. Which means I need a way for coworkers who live in different cities and states to get to know one another and stay connected."

That made sense.

"I also want to engage my people in team-building exercises, not just fun getaways. Except I want the team building to be organic. And I need a senior person to come in and plan events that will feel and play out naturally with my employees."

Though it all sounded like a blast, she wasn't looking for a job. So how come she felt unable to walk away from this conversation?

"If you'll commit to a year, in return I guarantee three assistant positions. You can live in one of the corporate apartments, so you don't have to move. Weekends are your own time. I promise not to call or text or need anything from you on Saturday or Sunday." He named the salary.

At the six-figure number, her heartbeat raced. She wanted to jump up and down. Except she played it cool. That was double her previous salary. With funds like that as a nest egg for her wedding venue, she would certainly succeed. "I don't know what to say."

"Think about it. Pray about it. Just don't say no—at least not yet." He maintained strong eye contact as he clasped his hands together under his chin in a pleading position. "Once you have a competent assistant, you can work four days a week. I know your wedding venue is a priority, but I think we can accomplish both at the same time." He gave her a swift nod, as though sealing the deal.

"Wow, Conrad. I don't know what to say."

"I knew I'd have to make it a pretty sweet deal to have any hope of interesting you." He shook her hand. "Laney, you have my number. Call or text me, preferably within the week."

Could she work for Conrad, still have her new business and enjoy a growing relationship with Ethan?

All this talk of assistants gave her an idea. Maybe she could hire an assistant in Serenity to meet with clients during the week when she was working in Dallas. Maybe this could work.

This was a great opportunity for her. Part of her had been petrified that she'd fail at her new business venture and end up homeless, just like her mother. What if this job—which she could probably do in her sleep—was a gift from God? She could bank the money for her start-up.

She spotted Ethan across the way. At the impromptu picnic, he'd discussed his quickie marriage to Joy and his poor decision-making skills. It sounded like Joy had talked Ethan into marriage. He clearly hadn't been thinking straight. She couldn't hold those actions against him, not after he'd shown himself to be such a great father, cowboy, brother and friend. The time since the picnic had only solidified her feelings for him.

She wove through partygoers, making her way to Ethan. But Laney worried that maybe he wasn't ready to move forward.

She loved Willow Creek Ranch and the transformation into a wedding venue. With the lease money, she could cover costs and take time to decide what she wanted to do. And with the year's salary from Conrad, she'd have the financial stability she'd always longed for.

On the plus side, she and Ethan would have the time to see if their developing feelings meant anything.

"Laney, thanks for doing all this for our parents." Walker McCaw stopped her.

"My pleasure. And thanks for booking the band." The sadness in his eyes almost made her want to cry. Even amid a celebration, the pain of losing his wife stood out.

"No prob. Everyone is having a great time."

"I think they are."

He turned to go.

"Wait. Walker, you work for Conrad Vaughn, right?" One of the two McCaws who had attended college, Walker lived in a cute little house in town.

"I do."

"Is he on the up-and-up?"

"Absolutely. Conrad is the most honest man I know. He follows through on whatever he says he's going to do."

"Thanks, Walker. I appreciate that."

He left as quickly as he'd arrived.

She took in the easy bantering, the carefree moments and the comforting hugs happening around the town square this evening. In the six weeks she'd been here, Serenity had been every bit as quaint as she remembered.

She loved the town, the slower pace of life, and of course, Ethan and the girls were simply the cherry on top. She'd missed this community. Missed having people care about her, people cheering her on. She wanted Serenity and everything Serenity stood for.

The money Conrad had offered her was an easy decision since her mother had stolen her identity and racked up credit card debt in Laney's name. She could still remember using every spare cent for three years to pay it off and clear her name. Part of her was still that broken girl, afraid to fall into debt of any kind.

She finally spotted Ethan again, chatting

with friends across the way, and she made a beeline for him. She'd been so busy doing the final preparations for the event that she had spent little time with him today. Once the party started, she'd had to make sure all the moving pieces were working. With Conrad's job offer bouncing around in her brain, she wanted to share the exciting news with Ethan. Each time she saw him, the pull was stronger.

A group of friends surrounded him, chatting. She eased next to him, getting close enough that he could slip his hand in hers. All night she'd longed to be by his side, enjoying the evening with him.

He captured her hand and squeezed while the friends said their goodbyes, a few of them smacking Ethan on his back as they left.

"Amazing party." He pulled her into the circle of his muscular arms. "Congratulations," he whispered into her ear and gave her a quick hug.

"Yes, it is going well." She surveyed the town square. Her gaze spied Conrad's lean frame and excitement bubbled in her chest. "Conrad Vaughn offered me a job." She bounced up on her toes, more enthusiastic now that she could share the news with Ethan.

"Really? I didn't realize you were looking for one." He released her hand.

"I'm not. He sought me out. Apparently he was impressed with this shindig." She was still shocked at his offer. "He offered me a corporate apartment and weekends off so I can focus on the wedding venue. He'll let me hire a staff, and once I get things rolling, I get Fridays off."

He stared at her as though disappointed instead of excited.

"Did I say I get weekends off? And it's a one-year commitment. I was thinking I could save the salary and use it for my new business. What do you think?" She could work in Dallas and start her venue without stretching herself too thin, right?

"I guess I thought you were starting your new business here in Serenity."

"Oh, I am. I think I can do both. Don't you?"

Was she being too selfish in considering this job? No, because Ethan worked a lot. If she was gone half of the week, they'd still have plenty of time together on the weekends. And by hiring an assistant here in Serenity, she wouldn't return from Dallas with a full plate.

"Sounds like a great offer." He gave her a tight smile.

The truth suddenly hit her. He didn't want her to take it. Given her childhood and her constant lack of funds, not accepting that enormous amount of easy money seemed risky. Conrad was offering her the opportunity to guarantee the success of her new business—and the stability she feared she might not have with this new venture.

"So you don't think I should take it?"

Couldn't he see the financial security this one-year gig would give her? How they'd see each other on weekends. That this opportunity would alleviate the stress she'd been feeling about the construction going over budget.

She braced herself for Ethan's response. Would he encourage her decision or place her in a box just like she'd seen unsupportive men do in the past?

She lifted her chin and waited.

Ethan felt like someone had just punched him in the gut. He schooled his features. "You should do what you want. You don't report to me." Her excitement was palpable, but it made him queasy.

"Well, I guess I thought…"

Yes, he thought so, too. Except, here she was, picking the city over him. Just like he had feared.

His hands were shaking. He knew she'd go. Could hear it in her voice and see it in her eyes, but that didn't take away the sorrow he'd feel for a long time coming over losing her. He swiped his eyes with the back of his hand. Did those evenings when they'd rocked on Alice and Arthur's porch swing mean nothing to her? They'd talked about life and hopes and dreams. Somehow, he had thought she was the one. The person God had made to complete him.

Just this past weekend, Laney had professed to falling in love with this sweet town. She was excited about starting a new business here. He'd thought he and the twins were part of the future she wanted. How could a job offer in Dallas interest her?

During their marriage, Joy always had one foot out the door. Seemed like Laney hadn't really meant it when she'd told him she planned to settle in Serenity.

Right now, it looked like she'd get her venue going and hire people to run it for her while she lived in Dallas.

He didn't want to stand in the way of Laney's career, fearful she would remain in Serenity because he expected her to and then be unhappy. Joy had told him that she felt trapped by marriage and children, so forcing Laney to stay would be a mistake.

When would he ever learn? The people who professed to love him deserted him. Period.

She took his hand. "Did I mention I'd get weekends off?"

What should he say? He loved her and wanted her here, but he'd tried to make Joy stay, and look where that had gotten him. He shook off her hand and scrubbed a palm over his face.

Ethan wanted Laney to choose Serenity. Because she loved him. Because she wanted a small town over city life.

If she remained here because he talked her into it, that would be disastrous. No. He would not sway her decision. This was her career, her life, and he would not stand in her way.

He lifted his chin. "It sounds like an amazing opportunity."

Right then, the twins descended upon them. He gathered them in his arms. This triple hug reminded him they were a unit, one that could never break. Except, before he knew it, they targeted the enemy and settled against Laney, asking her question after question about the party.

He clenched his jaw, afraid to say anything lest he tell her how much she meant to him, to the girls. No, she needed to make her own choices. If he knew one thing about Laney, it was that she didn't like conflict. She might be the type of person to agree so she didn't upset anyone. And if her heart was in the city and not here, he certainly didn't want to stifle her.

"Let's go, girls." He snatched Tori, but she wiggled away and into Laney's waiting arms.

Laney gazed up at him, unshed tears in her eyes. If he didn't say something right now, he'd lose her for good.

He pulled Zoe to him, but she scampered around him and landed at Laney's feet. It gutted him to see the agony in Laney's expression.

As though the girls understood what was happening, they wound their arms around Laney's legs, entrapping her.

He could see it in her eyes—she was leaving. He refused to stand between her and the city. He could not compete with a furnished apartment. A staff. A high salary. There was nothing left to say.

This was all too reminiscent of Joy's departure. No matter how hard or how much he loved someone, they wouldn't necessarily love him enough to stay. How had he dared hope for a future with her?

He should have known Laney would pick the city over him. Over a future with a small-town cattle rancher.

Their relationship was over.

Chapter Fifteen

When Ethan tossed her a steely glare that made her heart pause, Laney knew their relationship was over. He had needed a nanny. Period.

Well, she had needed a handyman, so they'd both gotten what they wanted. Except why did her chest hurt so much?

Zoe and Tori clung tight to her. Had they heard the whispered words? Or detected the animosity in the adults' voices?

That he wasn't excited about this short-term opportunity proved to her that she had almost neglected her own wants and put herself in a position to fail at her goals.

Laney had thought Ethan cared for her, maybe even loved her.

She untangled her hand from Tori as a heaviness settled in her chest. Why had she allowed herself to dream of happily-ever-after?

"Lane, Lane." Tori opened her arms. "Up, up."

What could she do? Laney picked up the sweet child and snuggled her tight, breathing in the little-girl smell she'd grown to adore. Was this their last moment together?

"Joy, Joy—look, Tori, Joy's here." Zoe's face lit up.

Tori scampered down to join her sister.

Laney's breath caught in her throat at Joy's arrival. She recognized the woman entering their circle from the one picture Ethan kept on the mantel. Her hair and makeup were perfect in that photo, just as they were today. Joy wore a short bright red dress. She came up to Ethan, then leaned in to kiss him on the cheek.

His gaze met Joy's and something passed between them.

Of course. They had a history. And twins together.

A heavy perfume, most likely expensive, hovered over the small group.

The evening, which had started out with such promise when Conrad made Laney the amazing offer, had gone downhill quickly. She knew she should leave, but she couldn't. Dumped by

Ethan right before his ex-wife returned to rec-oncile. Sounded like a horror movie.

Right then, Laney knew that even if they hadn't broken up, she'd walk away and give Joy the time to reconnect with Ethan, as well as the twins, without Laney hanging around. It was only fair. She would never stand in the way of parents reconciling.

Happiness should be swirling in her core, because the girls would now have both their parents, something Laney had longed for dur-ing her entire childhood. Her eyes brimmed with moisture that she vowed would not drip down her face.

Autumn joined the group and slid her arm around Laney's shoulders. "Joy." Her voice oozed with annoyance.

Joy lifted her chin. "Autumn." Their cool tones were identical.

"We're outta here." Autumn grabbed Laney's hand, and they strode away.

An invisible fist squeezed the breath out of her lungs. Joy had returned. And now Ethan and Joy would get their second chance. And the twins would get their mother.

She should be happy for them, but her heart ached.

"Great party, Laney." Autumn gave her hand

a squeeze. "Mom and Dad were super surprised. Did you see my mom cry?" Autumn's face fell as her eyes grew wide. "What's wrong?" She leaned in, concern covering her face.

Exhaustion and disappointment flared before Laney could control the almost-tears. "You saw. Joy's back."

When Ethan had turned quiet and judgmental after hearing about the job offer, it was clear she had misread what she thought was their growing relationship. But with Joy's arrival, none of that mattered. Whatever they had was over.

Her eyes burned with a mixture of sadness and loss.

"Oh, don't worry about her." Autumn waved her hand.

Don't worry about her? What?

Autumn knew how much Ethan meant to Laney. She tried to push her hurt feelings away.

They wove between groups of people chatting and eating. Everyone seemed to be having a wonderful time. As Laney took a plate, she realized she had no choice but to accept Conrad's offer. It would get her away from seeing Joy with Ethan and the twins. Laney wasn't sure she could handle that sight.

Lord, what should I do?

She'd sure miss everyone in town while she spent the next year in Dallas. Her heart sighed.

And what would happen to her wedding venue? Should she just sell?

Because the last thing she wanted was to live in a town where the love of her life was happily remarried to his children's mother.

Yes, she'd be pleased for them, but selfishly she didn't want to see it play out in front of her.

Ethan watched the love of his life leave as the twins clamored for the gifts Joy held.

He blinked. Why was Joy here? At a small-town event? The type of occasion she had always avoided during their time together. For a moment, he thought perhaps Autumn had invited her, but then he shook his head. No, Joy wasn't here to honor his parents. As usual, she probably wanted something.

"Joy, Joy, are those for us?" It broke his heart to see Joy buy off the girls every time she showed up. The twins equated Joy with gifts, not motherhood.

She'd insisted they call her Joy the first time she dropped by, and the girls never questioned it. They never asked why they didn't call her Mom. He'd been waiting for one of them to bring up the topic, but so far, they hadn't. Maybe their instincts told them that even though Joy had birthed them, she was not a proper mother.

"What are you doing here?" he grumbled.

"These are for you." She handed off the bags to Tori and Zoe like she thought they might bite.

The girls thanked her as they took the presents, tossed the sparkly white tissue paper to the side and grabbed some type of electronic devices from the smart, matte-black gift bags. "Can we show our friends?" Their eyes gleamed with excitement.

"As long as you pick up the garbage and throw it away." He motioned at the paper and bags littering the ground beneath their feet.

They grabbed every bit of gift material before leaving to show off their new toys.

Joy reached for him, her touch slithering up his arm. He stepped away. "What?" he growled.

Her eyebrows lifted. Slightly. Autumn had told him about the Botox. Joy's face now had a plastic glow about it.

"That's no way to treat a newly engaged woman." She thrust her left hand at him, sporting a diamond about the size of Texas.

"Congratulations?" He wasn't sure what response she was looking for.

He spied the twins across the park with their friends, showing off their expensive toys.

"Turns out you can find true love more than once in a lifetime." She gave him a sly grin. "I just wanted you to know I won't have the time to check in constantly with you and the girls anymore."

He could count on one hand the number of times she'd visited since she abandoned them. And a text every few Friday nights was not that difficult, since Joy rarely followed up on her initial inquiry, as though she cut and pasted her weekly check-in message.

"No problem." He looked over at the girls again. Though it was way past their bedtime, they played with their friends like they still had energy and stamina.

Joy grasped his upper arm, like she was desperate. "Listen, Ethan." Her voice had lowered. "Preston doesn't know about the girls. And since he has children from his prior two marriages, we've decided not to have kids." She frowned. "He's not fond of little ones."

Kind of like you.

"Anyway, I won't be able to call or text *at all* anymore." She held his gaze, as though trying to make sure he got her point.

Oh, he understood her perfectly. She didn't want the twins when they were babies, and she had no use for them now. Well, thankfully, they had him, an aunt, grandparents, a bevy of uncles and an entire church family to love and guide them.

"So, I just want to make it clear I don't want *you* to contact me, either. No matter what."

"I promise to never call or text again, if that's what you really want." She needn't worry, because Ethan didn't want to share this conversation with his girls. It would hurt them too much to know their mother cared more about herself than them.

His children deserved much more than Joy.

As Joy waltzed away, he realized he should have been kinder to Laney. She was nothing like Joy. Laney had never tried to take from the girls. She had always given so much. Repeatedly.

Yes, Laney was a good person, but she longed for the city. He heard it in her voice tonight.

It was best for everyone if he put Laney in his—and his girls'—rearview mirror lest anyone get hurt again.

The pain in his chest attested it was too late—he was deeply and forever in love. But maybe Tori and Zoe could bounce back from a Laney-less life quicker than he.

Early the next morning, in her summer-childhood bedroom, Laney zipped her suitcase closed and dropped it to the floor. *Dallas, here I come.* Instead of excitement, she was filled with dread.

The events of last night in the town square with Ethan returned. She squeezed the bridge of her nose to keep from crying. She had been disposable in her mother's life, in her ex-boyfriend's life and now in Ethan's.

A heaviness settled in her chest. Why did she allow herself to hope and dream? She wasn't worthy of being a part of a happy, functioning family. She knew that six weeks ago. Nothing had changed.

When she had heard Conrad's offer, never had she thought Ethan was about to dismiss her from his life. Except he had needed a nanny. The memory fisted in her chest. He had used her. Now he no longer had a need for her.

And of course Joy had returned.

Sorrow over leaving Ethan and the girls shattered Laney's heart.

What was she thinking, getting involved with Ethan? And now he had her heart.

She bumped her suitcase down the narrow stairwell and to the front door. With Joy back in the picture, she didn't want to be around. Laney had no option but to accept Conrad's offer and throw herself into his generous event-planning position.

Except, she wasn't sure she could walk through that door and drive away from Willow Creek Ranch. It just might break her.

As she glanced out the window, she spotted Autumn pulling into the drive.

No, Lord. If I don't leave now, I don't think I'll have the fortitude.

Autumn climbed the porch steps with huge to-go coffees and a pink box from Morning Grind in her hands.

The sweet gesture caused fresh tears to prick Laney's eyes, but she held them back. She had made her decision. Well, Ethan had made it for her. First he'd dismissed her. Then Joy had reappeared to reunite with him and the girls.

"Where are you going?" Autumn stood in the doorway.

"Taking the job in Dallas." She stared at her suitcase. Could she manhandle her belongings past her friend and escape before the conversation got too emotional?

Ethan deserved more than her. Someone complete, not a broken and wounded woman who'd never be able to get a relationship right.

The memory of Joy leaning in to kiss Ethan's cheek last night was burned into her mind.

Maybe Joy had changed. For her to take the step of coming back, that was huge. And to attend a small-town event by choice. Yes, Joy had changed.

A sheen of moisture glazed her eyes. Laney didn't *want* to go to Dallas. She yearned to settle right here in Serenity. Except now, with Joy back, she had no choice. She had to leave. He and the girls deserved a happily-ever-after with Joy. To build a proper family. And Laney had no desire to see all that happiness happen in real time.

Autumn's brows drew together. "You mean because Ethan got bent out of shape about the city job?" She rolled her eyes. "Give him a few days. He'll come around." She set down the doughnuts, then handed Laney a caramel macchiato, Laney's comfort drink.

A tear dribbled down her cheek at the good friend she'd found in Autumn. She leaned against a kitchen chair and took a sip, one sip, before she fled. Fled this conversation. Fled Ethan and Joy's renewed romance. Fled to the safety of Dallas and a job that wouldn't hurt her.

"A few days won't fix anything." How come Autumn was ignoring Joy's return? Her and Ethan's opportunity to become a family again.

The tantalizing smell of the doughnuts filled the kitchen. Laney tried to focus on her friend and not on the scent of deep-fried treats.

"Give him grace, Laney. He was probably upset when he heard about Conrad's offer. It came out of nowhere." She settled in a chair as though here for the entirety of their conversation and sipped her chai latte. "I know you find trusting hard, but I think Ethan deserves it. He's definitely worth a second chance."

Laney eyed the door. She wanted to leave, but a part of her longed to understand why Autumn was acting so calm about Joy's reappearance. "You don't get it. Joy is back. They are getting *their* second chance."

"Laney, I don't know why she was at the party last night, but I doubt very much that she has any interest in being a part of Ethan's or the girls' lives."

Her chest tightened. "You didn't see his face. And Tori and Zoe's excitement." No matter how painful leaving Ethan and the girls was, no matter how lonely and hollow her life in Dallas would feel, Ethan and the twins deserved a fresh start with Joy without Laney hanging around, possibly mucking things up.

Decision made, Laney rolled her luggage to the porch. "Listen, Autumn, can you monitor the renovation while I'm gone? Text me any questions with pictures, okay?" She'd have to make this formal, or maybe hire someone with more free time on their hands. But she couldn't worry about those details today. Not now.

Autumn stood, eyes wide. "Okay. When will you be back? Next weekend?"

Laney smiled at her friend, then lifted her drink. "Thanks so much. I appreciate this. Lock up when you leave?"

Why had she dreamed of a beautiful future with Ethan and the girls? She had made the same mistake as her mother by relying on a man for her happiness.

She never should have handed her heart to Ethan, because she knew better than to believe in love.

Chapter Sixteen

Saturday afternoon, Ethan collapsed in a recliner, hoping the twins were exhausted enough to take their naps today.

It had been a week since his parents' anniversary party. A week since Laney had informed him of Conrad's job offer. His heart remained bruised and battered.

After seven days, he'd thought his feelings for Laney would have diminished. The twins would stop asking for her. His chest wouldn't do a little dance every time he received a text because he thought that maybe, just maybe, it was from Laney.

When he discovered she'd left town the very next morning, at dawn, deserting him and the girls just like Joy, he realized he had been right.

Then the thought that had been niggling him

all week rose—maybe she'd left town because he'd been foolish, not because she wanted the job in Dallas. The two options were polar opposites. One meant he'd made a mistake he needed to apologize for. The other meant Laney loved the city more than him.

Even with his mother watching the girls again, nothing seemed to return to normal. Six weeks ago his life had been black-and-white, and then Laney arrived, bringing all the colors of the rainbow with her. She'd pushed him, made him a better person, a better parent. She wasn't just a nanny to the twins—no, she was so much more. She adored them, taught them, disciplined them with love and kindness.

If only he could redo his reaction at the anniversary party. He'd definitely tell her how much he loved her, more than he'd loved anyone. Ever. Then he'd plead with her to make a long-distance relationship work. Would she have stayed? Would she have gone to Dallas but remained committed to their relationship?

He'd never know, because she had left.

Had he pushed her away?

No. She probably didn't want him, and there was nothing he could do about it.

Autumn barged in through the screen door. "Have you begged Laney to forgive you yet?"

She leaned against the counter, arms crossed tight.

"Me? She was the one who left." He stepped into the kitchen, where Autumn remained, clearly annoyed.

She tossed him a look. Part grief, part disgust. "She only left because she wanted to give you and Joy your *second chance*." She pierced him with a glare, daring him to confess the truth.

He threw up his hands. "Everyone knows Joy shows up once in a while. It doesn't mean a thing. But Laney picked the city. Not us."

Though, in reality, Laney had simply informed him of a job offer. A part-time gig in Dallas. She'd told him she'd be home on the weekends. That it wouldn't last more than a year. But fear had taken hold of Ethan's emotions, and he'd lashed out because he'd been afraid she'd pick the city over him. He had treated Laney horribly.

"You didn't even try to fight for her." Annoyance laced Autumn's tone. "What was she supposed to do?"

He glared at his sister and hated how right she was. "She was supposed to go back to Willow Creek Ranch and give me a day to cool off." An ache pressed in on his heart. "Instead, she packed up, drove to Dallas and accepted the swanky job offer practically the same day. To me, that sounds like a future she embraced." He'd been so irked when he discovered her gone.

"Ethan, come on. Two wrongs make nothing right. You pushed her away." His sister fisted her hands at her sides. "Did you really expect her to stay in tiny Serenity with the two of you on the outs? With her thinking Joy was back in your life? How humiliating for her."

A desperation he'd never felt before rose under his ribs, leaving him hopeless for air. "All this time, I felt like the girls and I were a puzzle with a piece missing." He ran a hand down his face. "Laney completes us."

"Glad you finally figured that out. Now you better do something about it, because the girl doesn't run after the boy." Autumn pushed away from the counter, leaving as quickly as she'd arrived.

I better do something? What did Autumn mean? Laney had made her choice. His mind flitted to their argument at the anniversary party. To his quick assumption that she'd pick the city over him. And finally, to the moment Joy appeared and what Laney may have assumed at his ex-wife's arrival. Especially because the twins had appeared excited to see their mother, but in reality, it was Joy's gifts that put the gleam in their eyes.

Oh, no, what had he done?

His gaze snagged on his worn Bible. His disappointment over his failed marriage had driven a wedge between him and God. Thankfully, his renewed quiet time had led to peace and a repaired relationship with the Lord.

He bowed his head and prayed. For clarity. For wisdom. And for an obvious path to reconciliation with Laney.

The verse from Jeremiah came to mind about how God had a plan for Ethan. Plans to prosper and not harm him, plans to give him hope and a future. The verse he'd been clinging to for the past few weeks.

Was Laney part of God's plan for him? Until his hurtful words, he had thought so.

All week he had felt off-kilter. Maybe he'd text Laney. He grabbed his phone, then slid it to the counter. Maybe not. The wisest thing would be to wait for an open door.

He grabbed a soda from the fridge. When he closed the door, he saw a collage of pictures he'd collected over the past six weeks. Some of Laney. Some of him and Laney. And then a slew of the four of them, like a family. The family he'd always dreamed of, longed for.

She completed him. Completed his family.

He couldn't live without her. He stared out the window overlooking his prized cattle but didn't really see anything. The success of the ranch meant nothing if he couldn't share it with Laney.

A knock sounded from the screen door. He turned and saw his mother balancing a large casserole dish. He rushed to open the door for her.

The mouthwatering smell of his mother's homemade lasagna lifted into the air.

"I know it's hot out, but I brought you some dinner." She placed the food on the counter, then turned and froze. "What's wrong?"

He looked at his mother, the one person in the world he could be real with. "How come I'm never first choice?"

She paused and cocked her head. "Are you talking about your birth mother? Because if so, stop right there." She crossed the room and settled on a bar stool. "Betty knew she couldn't be a proper parent. She can barely take care of herself. So she asked people she loved to raise you. Those choices changed your life, and ours, for the better. And deep down you know it."

Gratitude thrummed through him. He appreciated his parents. Not only because of everything they'd done for him and the ways they always encouraged him, but they never made him feel second best—that had been all his doing. "But what about Joy? Laney?"

"We tried to tell you how selfish Joy was. But there was no convincing you otherwise. The blessing is that she left before the girls formed a strong memory of her. Other than her quick visits, she cut her ties completely. Yes, you think her leaving was cruel, but frankly, I see that as a blessing, because the girls have a fresh start. No actual memories of their disinterested birth mother. Just a woman who shows up with gifts every once in a while, and now apparently never again."

"You say that like it was easy for me to handle having her walk out on us."

His mother came to the kitchen and side-hugged him. "You've told me before that once she learned of her pregnancy, she pulled away from you. By the time she left, she felt like a stranger."

"Yes, the romance Joy and I shared was short-lived." His birth mother didn't want him. His ex-wife didn't want him. And now he'd pushed Laney away. "I don't know what to do, Mom. I overreacted last week. And now Laney's gone."

"Don't let your fear of the past repeating stop you from working this out with Laney." She settled in a kitchen chair. "The question is, what are you going to do about it?"

Ethan had done too much on his own strength. "I'm going to wait for God to direct my steps." For however long that would be. He glanced at the lasagna. "Why'd you bring dinner? You know I have the day off. I can feed the girls myself. You do too much for us as it is."

"Earlier today I felt the need to make the girls dinner. And as I walked over just now, God impressed on me to offer to watch Tori and Zoe this weekend." Her eyes teared. "I don't know why. I mean, you don't have any plans, but I'm just being obedient."

He gulped. *Thank You, Lord.* He didn't have plans, but he sure could make some.

If he didn't go after Laney, he would always wonder, *what if?*

"I'm scared, Mom," he whispered as his gut tightened.

His mother wrapped him in a hug. "Doing the right thing may be hard. But it is always for the best."

He nodded. He refused to be like his birth mother and his ex-wife, who'd betrayed him by choosing not to stay and love him. Today, he chose to trust. To love. To stay.

"I'm going to Dallas."

In the Dallas corporate apartment, Laney set the white container of sweet-and-sour chicken next to the beef with broccoli on the leather ottoman. The tangy smells of the Chinese food lifted into the air, but her thoughts were on Ethan. She settled on the carpet to eat her boring leftovers in front of some mindless television.

Not too long ago, Laney would have relished a free Saturday afternoon. But after six weeks with Ethan, there was no place she'd rather be than in Serenity. With Ethan. And the twins.

But he had made it clear he didn't want her anymore.

Her phone rang. It was her friend Rose.

"How'd your first week go?"

Laney sighed. "I never thought I'd tire of the corporate world, but I have."

"Tell me."

"I called Emily last weekend when I arrived. Remember her? She was so excited about helping me at CV Security that she packed a bag and came right up. She stayed in a hotel, and we brainstormed all sorts of things." A week that

Laney would have relished a mere two months ago, but it had left her feeling empty and sad. "I just might promote her and return to Serenity."

"I still can't believe that tiny town didn't bore you." Rose huffed.

"Oh, Rose, I can't tell you how wonderful Serenity is." Even across the miles, she could tell her friend had scrunched up her face. "It was so refreshing. I actually slept through the night and woke up rejuvenated."

"I still can't believe that. Sounds like a dream." Both she and Rose had been fitful sleepers ever since they'd met. "So, you really liked it there? You weren't just putting up with it because you started your wedding venue there?"

"I loved it." All week she had prayed for God to take away her feelings for Ethan. But instead she felt a peace about him having her full heart. No matter how much she tried to hold back, she loved him. And the girls. Working in Dallas wouldn't change that. "I'm thinking of going back. For good."

"What about Conrad?"

"His biggest concern was trust, and I know and trust Emily. She'll do a great job for him."

"I can't forget when you told me about that surprise workday where the townspeople showed up to help with the renovations. Now you have me dreaming of relocating to the middle of nowhere."

"Come up to Serenity. I'd love to have you there." She picked up an egg roll from her plate. "The good thing about small towns is that everyone knows everything about you. But that's also the bad thing. I know Ethan won't welcome me back. And I'm unsure what the residents' reaction will be." She pushed her plate away, no longer hungry.

"What does it matter what Ethan thinks or feels? If Serenity is your home, go back."

Pressure pounded behind her eyes, but Laney refused to give in and cry. Again.

"Honestly, I miss the slower pace of Serenity," she shared. "I crave time with the twins and ranch life. And I long for Ethan."

Her heart was at the ranch—and in Ethan's capable hands. She was sick of trying to strive for her independence when, in actuality, all she wanted was to be back in Ethan's arms. To mother Zoe and Tori. To live in Serenity and be part of the close and supportive community. Not that he wanted her. Now that he had Joy back.

Rose sucked in a breath. "You're in love."

She refused to say the *L* word. It was too late

for a relationship with Ethan. That was in the past. "The problem is that I don't want to put Ethan in an uncomfortable position. I mean, he clearly doesn't care for me like I do for him."

She missed Serenity and everything about it. If only she could figure out a way to move back to Willow Creek Ranch and not make it awkward between her and Ethan, she would scurry back in a heartbeat.

"You don't know that."

"Yes, I do. You didn't see his face. He's still in love with his ex."

"Oh, Laney, I don't think it's over between you and Ethan," Rose said. "From everything you told me about Joy, I can't believe she was there to win Ethan back."

"Really?" At the anniversary party, Ethan had appeared enthusiastic when he spotted Joy. But had Laney read his expression wrong? Maybe. Hope grew.

"It sounds like, during that silly squabble—and I truly think that's all it was—you pushed his buttons and he pushed yours. Seems like you both struggle with fear."

Rose spoke words of wisdom. Even though love could hurt, Laney now knew that love was better than fear. If she got the opportunity again, she'd choose love and trust over fear and running.

Ethan had cared for Laney, and he was nothing like the men her mother attracted. So if Laney were to get a second chance with Ethan, she wouldn't hesitate. She'd grab on and cherish him forever.

After filling the tank with gas, Ethan settled in his truck. What if Laney rejected him when he arrived in Dallas? Had he hurt her too much to repair? What if she loved being back in the city?

He rubbed a hand over his scruffy chin, second-guessing not shaving before he left. Well, at least he had showered. After he sipped his coffee, he pulled onto the highway and eased into traffic. He wanted Laney to forgive him and be willing to give their relationship another shot.

He steeled his jittery nerves as he finally turned into her apartment complex in Dallas. Autumn had given him the address. Among a sea of polished new sedans, minivans and sports cars, he slid his banged-up dusty truck into a parking spot.

He stepped onto the pavement, stretched his back and stared at the concrete jungle Laney adored. And tried not to judge. How could anyone live with all this concrete? All these people? No pastures or wide-open spaces? No clean air to breathe.

As he rode the elevator to the top-floor apartment, he prayed for the right words to express himself.

He knocked on her door and then palmed his Stetson. Silence. Maybe she wasn't here? Maybe she was working at an event this evening.

Oh, he hoped she was here, or coming back soon. He desperately wanted to share his heart with the woman he loved.

After the longest minute of his life, the door cracked open. The opening was wide enough to see her, but she didn't invite him in. Laney wore yoga pants that flared at the bottom and a CV Security sweatshirt. She fingered her wavy hair, a pensive look on her face. She looked absolutely adorable.

"Am I interrupting?" Her nearness made his senses spin. Clearly, she didn't want him in her apartment.

From the stiff features on her face, she didn't plan on speaking. After the way he had treated her, he didn't blame her.

As the coffee in his stomach churned, he

worked up his courage. "I'm here to apologize. I overreacted, and I'm so sorry." His words came out quick, frantic.

"Sorry about what?"

Okay. He deserved that. *Explain away, man, and make it good.* "Dismissing you. Assuming you'd choose the city over me. I was an idiot."

Her eyes seemed to soften a little. Did the door open a tiny bit more?

Adrenaline coursed through his body as he held on to hope that she would forgive him. Give him another chance.

She nibbled her lower lip. "How are things going with Joy?"

He cocked his head, then remembered Laney had seen Joy's little show last week. "She's getting remarried." He shared everything Joy had told him.

Laney clapped her fingers to her mouth. "Oh, no! Tori and Zoe must be heartbroken."

"Not really. I've been truthful with them from the get-go. She drops in from time to time, but gives them toys, not love and affection." He twirled his Stetson in his hands.

"I didn't know that. Come in, come in." She tugged his arm and shut the door behind him.

He had made it into the apartment.

Emotions exploded in his chest. He stopped

her in the expansive entryway, clad in mirrors and crystals and white wood, and took her soft hands in his.

Time to grovel. "When I heard about this job in the city, it scared me. Made me think of the demise of my relationship with Joy. So I lashed out." He licked his parched lips and continued. "But you aren't Joy. And if working for Conrad for a year will fatten your bank account enough to ease your financial stress, I support that."

He wanted her business to succeed, but most of all, he wanted to spend the rest of his life with her.

Laney's handsome cowboy was here. Her body trembled with nerves.

His dark hair was messy, as though he'd been running his fingers through it. Worry lines etched on his forehead.

Had Ethan really just apologized? Had he just pursued her all the way from Serenity? Hope for the future filled her.

Her heart fluttered. "Where are my manners? Come on in." She strode to the living area.

As he pulled off his dusty cowboy hat, his muscular arm flexed. He laid it on the stainless-steel counter. "Nice place." When he walked in, he filled the space.

She glanced around the modern room, adorned with chrome and glass, and shrugged. The decorator had apparently gone for the industrial look. To her, it felt cold and unwelcoming.

He settled on the couch, dwarfing the square-armed white leather piece.

She perched on the other end, drawing her knees up to her chest and wrapping her arms around them. She'd wait. The pain under her rib cage was still battered and bruised. He deserved to grovel a little.

His eyes fixed on her intensely. "Like I said, I am so sorry. I overreacted." His gaze dropped to the ground before returning to her face. Searching. "Can you ever forgive me?"

Her heart thudded dangerously. She still couldn't believe Ethan was here. In her apartment. In Dallas. Apologizing. Could she actually get the man, children and white picket fence of her dreams? "I absolutely forgive you, Ethan. I lashed out at you as well, and for that, I'm sorry."

With her pronouncement, his shoulders relaxed. He shifted closer to her.

"I was afraid." His Adam's apple bobbed.

"Afraid that you'd pick the city over me. Afraid that your career was more important than us. I am so sorry."

"I assume you were also protecting your girls from getting hurt again. And this time they'd remember me, and the loss would hurt more."

"That, too."

"I understand. I was afraid I was relying on a man—you—instead of *my* power. But then God reminded me that I need to rely on Him."

"Amen. How's the new job going?"

"Let's just say that six weeks in the country tamed me. I'm no longer made for the city." As she slid a little closer to him, she could smell the spice of his cologne.

His eyes sparkled. "It'd be a lie to say I was sorry to hear that." He took her hand. "The girls miss you."

"Only the girls?"

He chuckled and squeezed her hand. "I miss you terribly. My life has felt empty since you left." He pressed his lips to her forehead. "I love you, Laney." The words came out so soft she almost didn't hear them.

Her heart seemed to stop, then began pounding furiously at his declaration. "You do?"

"I do. Laney, I want to spend forever with you." He brushed her cheek with his thumb. "I made a mistake letting you leave. Now I know I can't live without you."

Her breath quickened. Yes, she had run away from Ethan when things got hard. But God had shown her the error of her ways. God had worked in Ethan's heart to help him accept he couldn't control everything. Then He spurred Ethan to come and fight for her. To show her what true love was.

"You're making me believe in happily-ever-afters." She reached out and drew her fingers along the rough stubble of his chin. One of his many attractive features. "I don't want to stay in Dallas, even if it's only part-time. And with the McCaws leasing the land, I'll be able to start my wedding venue with a positive cash flow. It'll be tight, but I believe it'll work."

He grinned. "Boy, am I relieved to hear that." He ran his knuckle along her jawline. She delighted at the affection.

"This week in the city has made me realize how much I loved the country. The wide-open spaces. The fresh air. Willow Creek Ranch. The twins. You." She wrapped her arms around him. "Ethan, I love you. So much."

He touched his lips to hers, the whiskers on his chin rough against her skin. It felt like home and a promise of forever.

He pulled away, then pressed his forehead to hers. "Are you sure the ranch life won't be too boring for you?"

She couldn't wait for the next day and the next and the next. She might be walking into an unknown future, but with Ethan, she'd walk anywhere. Even if it meant depending on someone else. Because Ethan made her happier than she'd ever been before.

"Wherever you and the girls are, that's my home."

Epilogue

A satisfied smile spread over her lips as Laney padded down the hall to start the coffee brewing. Oh, how she loved her new life.

She rounded the corner and caught Zoe tugging Tori away from the enormous gift draped in festive plastic. Pine scent lingered in the space from the gigantic Christmas tree in the corner.

Their identical reindeer pajamas were adorable but a little snug. Next year she'd purchase new ones. Maybe she'd get all four of them matching sleepwear.

"No, Tori, no touch." Zoe all but stomped her foot in frustration at her twin.

Laney's chest warmed at the vision. Seven months ago, she never would have envisioned her white-picket-fence dream would come true. Her very own happily-ever-after.

A floorboard creaked. From behind, Ethan wrapped her in a hug. "Merry Christmas, Mrs. McCaw." He kissed her cheek.

At her giggle, the twins turned to them. "Mommy, Daddy," they squealed and rushed over to squeeze their parents' legs.

"Can we open the big thing?" Tori pointed to the covered toy kitchen they'd spent half the night assembling, the reason she needed caffeine right now. At the moment, a giant piece of red plastic dotted with white snowflakes covered the beautiful vintage wooden kitchen set.

She'd lived with their plastic playhouse monstrosity on the patio for a month now. She'd insisted their next large play item be wood. And classic.

Ethan ruffled Tori's mess of hair. "Stockings first, kiddo."

The twins rushed to the mantel and waited for their father to unhook the stockings from the horseshoe-shaped hangers.

Laney settled on the couch. The sweet sight in front of her made her heart sing. Ethan joined her, and they sat together as the girls frantically pulled out pieces of candy and tiny wrapped presents. A mound of tissue paper, candy wrappers and wrapping paper grew between them.

The memory of him apologizing and wooing her in that Dallas corporate apartment only five months ago was still clear in her mind. She'd thought they were over. Boy, had she been wrong.

Laney leaned her head against his shoulder. "I still can't believe you came after me this summer."

"For you, anything." He pressed a kiss against her forehead.

"And the romantic proposal at the family bonfire over Labor Day weekend." She released a satisfied sigh. Everyone had been there. All of Ethan's siblings had shown up. After dinner and s'mores, the fire had grown tall. The evening had been simply perfect. And then the proposal.

"I'm glad you said yes." After the proposal, he'd shared how he hadn't been confident she'd accept. She'd responded with a kiss to squelch any of his lingering doubts.

Laney lifted her hand and admired her engagement ring. Two small stones, one pink and one purple to acknowledge each girl, flanked the center diamond. The rose-gold band swirled in a never-ending fashion. Ethan had informed her it represented forever. *Yes, please.*

She loved that he had put such thought into a piece of jewelry. She would have agreed to marry him no matter what, but this thoughtful ring had made the moment even more special.

The girls shrieked at the last item they pulled from their stockings. Pink and purple bandannas.

Laney grinned. It had surprised her to discover they didn't own bandannas. How could they be cowgirls without bandannas?

They clumsily tried to tie them on.

"Come over here. Let me."

Their eyes lit up as they rushed to her.

"I can't believe we're married. And I'm a mother," she whispered to Ethan.

"Happy one-month anniversary." He kissed her. Long and gentle, with the promise of more.

Tori squeezed between them. Laney reached down and tied Zoe's pink then Tori's purple bandanna around their necks.

"We cowgirls."

Laney kissed the top of their heads, their curly hair tickling her nose. "I can't believe it's only been a month."

"It was a perfect day," Ethan said.

"We was pretty, Daddy," Zoe stated.

"Yup. Dressed in pretty frills and cowboy boots, you two were darling." He tickled each under their chins, and they erupted in laughter.

"And you were stunning." His cocoa eyes twinkled at Laney.

The day had been perfect—the first wedding at her venue.

They'd held their twilight ceremony at the bluff overlooking the creek. Twinkle lights had been strung up all over the area, creating a romantic ambience. Perfect.

A few weeks later, she had hosted Rose's wedding. The venue had been booked since she opened, and Laney continued getting emails and calls.

"Gifts?" Tori asked.

"Yes," Ethan relented.

"Yay." Zoe and Tori climbed up to their laps and hugged them, making the Tori-and-Zoe sandwich, which they'd named the evening of their engagement.

"Thank you for the bandanna," Zoe stated.

"Yes, me, too. I love it," Tori said. "I love you, Mommy." She pressed her forehead against Laney's.

"Me, too." Zoe squished her face to join in.

Happy tears filled Laney's eyes as the twins clambered down and rushed to the stacked gifts under the tree. Her heart soared like a helium balloon for her new family. She'd never thought she'd be a mother, but Tori and Zoe had stormed into her life and she'd fallen in love with them.

After the girls unwrapped their last gift, an empty box with the picture of a bounce house on it, they cocked their heads in the couch's direction.

"To the garage," Ethan said.

Laney couldn't stop giggling. She couldn't wait for their response when they spotted the inflated castle plugged in and ready to use.

The girls scrambled down the hall and into the garage. At their rambunctious squeals, Laney covered her ears and leaned her head against her husband's sturdy shoulder as the girls bounced and screamed with glee.

Laney had it all.

The family she'd always dreamed of.

She thanked God for bringing her to Serenity at just the right time to meet the man of her dreams—and the children who needed her as much as she needed them.

* * * * *

Dear Reader,

Thank you for joining me at the Triple C Ranch in Serenity, Texas. The small town and wide-open spaces were inspired by my childhood. I pedaled my bike all over the place, gleefully rode horses whenever I could and spent every daylight hour playing outside.

Ethan and Laney's sweet story is about God redeeming our past, even when all we see are mistakes. The couple's journey teaches them to trust again and embrace their identity found in Christ. It is only when they let go of their past and accept God's redemption that they can seize their chance at love.

I would love to connect with you. Drop me a note at heidimain.com. While there, you can sign up for my newsletter for giveaways, news and yummy recipes.

Hugs,
Heidi

Get 4 FREE REWARDS!

We'll send you 2 FREE Books <u>plus</u> 2 FREE Mystery Gifts.

FREE Value Over $20

Both the **Love Inspired®** and **Love Inspired® Suspense** series feature compelling novels filled with inspirational romance, faith, forgiveness, and hope.

YES! Please send me 2 FREE novels from the Love Inspired or Love Inspired Suspense series and my 2 FREE gifts (gifts are worth about $10 retail). After receiving them, if I don't wish to receive any more books, I can return the shipping statement marked "cancel." If I don't cancel, I will receive 6 brand-new Love Inspired Larger-Print books or Love Inspired Suspense Larger-Print books every month and be billed just $6.24 each in the U.S. or $6.49 each in Canada. That is a savings of at least 17% off the cover price. It's quite a bargain! Shipping and handling is just 50¢ per book in the U.S. and $1.25 per book in Canada.* I understand that accepting the 2 free books and gifts places me under no obligation to buy anything. I can always return a shipment and cancel at any time by calling the number below. The free books and gifts are mine to keep no matter what I decide.

Choose one: ☐ **Love Inspired**
Larger-Print
(122/322 IDN GRDF)

☐ **Love Inspired Suspense**
Larger-Print
(107/307 IDN GRDF)

Name (please print)

Address   Apt. #

City   State/Province   Zip/Postal Code

Email: Please check this box ☐ if you would like to receive newsletters and promotional emails from Harlequin Enterprises ULC and its affiliates. You can unsubscribe anytime.

Mail to the **Harlequin Reader Service:**
IN U.S.A.: P.O. Box 1341, Buffalo, NY 14240-8531
IN CANADA: P.O. Box 603, Fort Erie, Ontario L2A 5X3

Want to try 2 free books from another series! Call 1-800-873-8635 or visit www.ReaderService.com.

---

*Terms and prices subject to change without notice. Prices do not include sales taxes, which will be charged (if applicable) based on your state or country of residence. Canadian residents will be charged applicable taxes. Offer not valid in Quebec. This offer is limited to one order per household. Books received may not be as shown. Not valid for current subscribers to the Love Inspired or Love Inspired Suspense series. All orders subject to approval. Credit or debit balances in a customer's account(s) may be offset by any other outstanding balance owed by or to the customer. Please allow 4 to 6 weeks for delivery. Offer available while quantities last.

Your Privacy—Your information is being collected by Harlequin Enterprises ULC, operating as Harlequin Reader Service. For a complete summary of the information we collect, how we use this information and to whom it is disclosed, please visit our privacy notice located at corporate.harlequin.com/privacy-notice. From time to time we may also exchange your personal information with reputable third parties. If you wish to opt out of this sharing of your personal information, please visit readerservice.com/consumerschoice or call 1-800-873-8635. **Notice to California Residents**—Under California law, you have specific rights to control and access your data. For more information on these rights and how to exercise them, visit corporate.harlequin.com/california-privacy.

LIRLIS22R2

Get 4 FREE REWARDS!

We'll send you 2 FREE Books plus 2 FREE Mystery Gifts.

Heir to the Ranch — MELISSA SENATE

More Than a Temporary Family — MARIE FERRARELLA

The Cowboy's Unlikely Match — Lisa Childs

The Mayor's Baby Surprise — Anna J. Stewart

FREE Value Over **$20**

Both the **Harlequin® Special Edition** and **Harlequin® Heartwarming™** series feature compelling novels filled with stories of love and strength where the bonds of friendship, family and community unite.

YES! Please send me 2 FREE novels from the Harlequin Special Edition or Harlequin Heartwarming series and my 2 FREE gifts (gifts are worth about $10 retail). After receiving them, if I don't wish to receive any more books, I can return the shipping statement marked "cancel." If I don't cancel, I will receive 6 brand-new Harlequin Special Edition books every month and be billed just $5.24 each in the U.S. or $5.99 each in Canada, a savings of at least 13% off the cover price or 4 brand-new Harlequin Heartwarming Larger-Print books every month and be billed just $5.99 each in the U.S. or $6.49 each in Canada, a savings of at least 20% off the cover price. It's quite a bargain! Shipping and handling is just 50¢ per book in the U.S. and $1.25 per book in Canada.* I understand that accepting the 2 free books and gifts places me under no obligation to buy anything. I can always return a shipment and cancel at any time by calling the number below. The free books and gifts are mine to keep no matter what I decide.

Choose one: ☐ **Harlequin Special Edition**
(235/335 HDN GRCQ)
☐ **Harlequin Heartwarming Larger-Print**
(161/361 HDN GRC3)

Name (please print)

Address   Apt. #

City   State/Province   Zip/Postal Code

Email: Please check this box ☐ if you would like to receive newsletters and promotional emails from Harlequin Enterprises ULC and its affiliates. You can unsubscribe anytime.

Mail to the **Harlequin Reader Service:**
IN U.S.A.: P.O. Box 1341, Buffalo, NY 14240-8531
IN CANADA: P.O. Box 603, Fort Erie, Ontario L2A 5X3

Want to try 2 free books from another series! Call 1-800-873-8635 or visit www.ReaderService.com.

HSEHW22R2

COUNTRY LEGACY COLLECTION

19 FREE BOOKS IN ALL!

Cowboys, adventure and romance await you in this new collection! Enjoy superb reading all year long with books by bestselling authors like Diana Palmer, Sasha Summers and Marie Ferrarella!